THE CRACKERJACK

crack-er-jack...a person that shows marked ability or excellence

A NOVEL BY

ROBERT M. DAVIS

THE CRACKERJACK

ISBN: 978-1-61170-278-1

This book is a work of fiction. Any references to historical events, real people, or real places are used fictitiously. Other names, characters, places, events, and incidents are products of the authors imagination, and any resemblance to actual events or places or persons, living or dead, is entirely coincidental.

Cover designed and illustrated by Bob Archibald.

Published by:

 Robertson Publishing™
www.RobertsonPublishing.com

Printed in the USA and UK on acid-free paper.

Also by Robert M. Davis:

> *The Ticker*
> *Will to Kill*
> *When The Enemy is You.*

To purchase books go to:

amazon.com
barnesandnoble.com
www.rp–author.com/robertdavis

DEDICATION

To Joanne, Brian, Kelli & Dylan.

CHAPTER ONE

Jackson bumped his leg into a body that was dead to the world. Sometime during the night his younger brother crawled into bed with him. Jim's breathing was deep and steady. Maybe Jim needed the security of his twelve year old brother after a bad dream. The boy could sleep through a hurricane. He was lucky that way. Their parents were at it again, arguing in the kitchen.

The walls of their small West Virginia farmhouse were cracker thin. A whisper was no more private than a shout. Jackson buried his head into the pillow. His dad spit out a swear word Jackson wasn't supposed to know the meaning of or say. The type of word his mother forbid in her house.

An eyelid crept open. Daylight had not yet pierced its presence through the gaps of a hanging sheet that served as a makeshift curtain for the bedroom window. The only clock in the house was a mute cuckoo in the living room - a previous year prize his father won for being 1958 salesman of the year. It was too early in the day for a man to be liquored up, but his father wasn't like most men. He was still drunk from the night before.

Jackson curled his knees into his stomach. Every time his parents argued his gut bothered him. He willed himself to go back to sleep. Maybe, when he woke up again his father would be miles away from the house shooting critters. Or passed out on the floor where the family could walk around him like a piece of furniture that snored.

"I don't give a Goddamn what you say, woman," his father bellowed. "I'm taking Jackson squirrel huntin' with me. A man has the right to go huntin' with his oldest son anytime he damn well pleases. Don't even start sassin' me about him missin' school. If he ain't playin' baseball, all the boy does is sit next to the radio readin' or studyin' them stupid baseball cards. School don't teach them nothin' about life, like puttin' food on the table and clothes on their

1

backs. You're raisin' two sissy boys, Ellie. Wake Jackson up now. If you don't, I will and he won't like it."

One of Jackson's parents bumped into the closed bedroom door. Jackson's head bounced up from the pillow. Jim didn't stir. Jackson knew from experience what would happen next. His father never left his mother much of an option. She usually let her husband have his way. Bad things would happen if she didn't.

"Keep your voice down, Emmett," his mom said. "You're not taking Jackson anywhere. You hear me? This is a school day. He's not going to miss another class because you want a hunting partner. This is one fight you aren't going to win. I mean it. Take your rifle outside. I'll brew you some coffee and bring it to you."

"Don't want no friggin' coffee. I've given you fair warning, Ellie. Get outta my way."

"Jackson isn't going hunting with you. Not in your condition."

Jackson sat up. Noise from his churning stomach offset the eerie silence in the kitchen.

He vaulted out of bed. If he volunteered to go hunting with his father, maybe he could save his mother from another beating, even if he had to take the pounding for her.

A .22 caliber rifle shot rang out from the kitchen, followed by a metallic ping. Jim turned in his sleep. Jackson held his breath and stared at the door.

"Say something, mom," Jackson whispered. Did his father really shoot his mother? "Please say something. Please..."

Jackson jumped when the bedroom door flew open. His mother rushed into the room and made a beeline to the far wall next to Jim's empty bed. He blew out a relieved breath. She jerked the shotgun from two hooks embedded into the wall. His mother was tiny compared to other women, but strong. She set a mulish jaw, carried the gun with both hands as if it were weightless, and marched to the door. Jackson moved into her pathway and pushed his palms at her. His stomach was on fire. How could he stop her?

"Go back to bed, Jackson," she ordered.

"But, but, Mom. He'll hurt you. Please let me go hunting with him. I'll be okay."

"Do as I say, Jackson." Her eyes squinted into slits. "No human, animal, or tree is safe when that man is under the influence. He just shot up the stove."

Jackson hesitated, then stepped aside. The door closed behind her. He sat on the bed, shaking. His hands and bare feet were icy cold. What should he do? He always obeyed his mother. She could be tough on her boys, but her tough wasn't mean like his father. How many times had Jackson heard his mother say, "One Emmett Kingman in this world is bad enough. No need to raise two more like to him."

His father growled several cuss words at his mother, followed by a threat to give her and the boys the beating of their lives. Then it got quiet. Jim mumbled in his sleep. Jackson learned at an early age how to read the temperature of his father's unstable moods when he was sober. But there was no telling what the man would do when he was on the bottle.

One metal click followed another - his father's Zippo lighter opening and closing. The scent of tobacco smoke came next. Maybe a cigarette would calm his father down.

"Emmett, if you take one more step, as God is my witness, I will shoot you."

His father coughed out a throaty smoker's laugh. A cruel, daring cackle Jackson had never heard before. He ran to the door. If he disobeyed his mother just this once...

"You ain't never pulled a trigger in your life, Ellie." His father laughed again. "We both know you don't have the grits to shoot me. Now, get outta my way, bitch."

KA-BOOM.

* * * * *

Jackson didn't remember entering the kitchen. One instant he was running towards the door, the next moment he was standing with his mother. His ears were ringing. Jim's shouts from the bedroom sounded as if they were coming from the nearest neighbor's house. His mother leaned the shotgun against the wall.

Smoke hovered near the ceiling. Gun powder fouled the room's air. A lit cigarette smoldered on the linoleum floor. Puddles of blood surrounded his prone father. A soft whistle wheezed from the still body peppered with numerous buckshot holes.

Tears spilled down Jackson's cheeks. A hand went to his lips to hold back bile rushing from an empty stomach. He was almost as tall as his mother. Her steely grey eyes told him her wits were in working order.

"Now don't you cry, boy." His mother grabbed Jackson's shoulders and shook him to attention. "Evil is evil. Your daddy is a sick man. Once he's inebriated, the devil in him takes over. He has abused this family long enough. What happened has nothing to do with you. It's nobody's fault but his own." She cupped a fist under his chin. "Get some clothes on. Run to the Zorn's house. They've got the nearest phone. Have them call for an ambulance and the sheriff. Go on now, get dressed."

Jim stumbled into the room. He stared at his father's body with an open mouth. His mother wrapped an arm around him, pushing his face into her side.

Jackson pulled on a pair of jeans and a shirt over his pajamas. His fingers trembled something awful, making it difficult to secure buttons through the button holes. He floated into the kitchen and headed to the back door. Something pulled on his shirt sleeve; his mother's fingers.

"There's snow on the ground, Jackson. Put your shoes on. And a jacket. Hurry, son."

* * * * *

A sheet with dark red splotches covered his father from muddy boots to hunting hat by the time Jackson returned from the half-mile roundtrip. He was out of breath. A whiff of death had replaced the gun powder odor. Jim was back in bed sucking his thumb. A distant siren prompted Jackson to close the bedroom door.

His mother sat at the kitchen table. Her vacant eyes stared at the bullet hole in the stove. She was still wearing a light blue housecoat and leather moccasin slippers. Her morning hair was uncombed. She lifted up an empty coffee mug and sipped air.

Jackson picked at his fingertips. A mixture of sad and glad gripped his soul. His protective mother had said it wasn't his fault.

It sure didn't feel that way. If he had disobeyed her and gone hunting, his father would be alive. What was the Kingman family going to do without his father's patchy income now he was dead and gone? Sober, Emmett Kingman and his third grade education could be a personable, glib-talking salesman. Heck, he even won a trip to Mexico City for two. At the very least, his father could provide food, clothes, and a roof over their heads by working in a paint store and selling Electrolux vacuum cleaners door to door. His mother would have to find work. If Jackson was a few years older, his destiny would be in the coal mines. It was no secret working the mines usually meant an early trip to the grave.

Tires skidded to a stop in the dirt driveway. A deputy sheriff entered through the kitchen door without knocking. He moved to an area on the floor with no blood and lifted the sheet. He made a face, like a man not expecting Tabasco Sauce mixed in with his scrambled eggs. The deputy studied the body and rifle, then lowered the sheet. His eyes fixed on the only other living adult in the room.

"Can you tell me what happened, ma'am?" the deputy asked.

"I shot him." Her expression didn't change. "He was drunk as a bird on berries and wanted to take our son out hunting this morning. I told him I'd shoot him if he took one more step towards the boy's room." She rose from the chair, went to Jackson and rubbed his arms with her hands. "I lied, deputy. Truth is, I gave my husband two steps before I shot him. What would you have done if Jackson was your son?"

Jackson couldn't stop shivering. His mother's warming touch didn't quell the tremors. He had failed both of his parents. Would the guilt clinging to him like a bloodsucking leech ever go away?

CHAPTER TWO

Jackson's stomach bounced after Judge Lane, sitting behind a huge oak desk, peeked up from a file resting on the desktop and peered at Jackson, then his brother Jim sitting on the other side of his mother. Was the judge trying to put a face to the printed names? Jackson released a silent breath when the judge's eyes returned to the file.

Judge Lane's chambers was a carpenter's dream; hardwood floors, dark wood paneling, wood chairs, wood file cabinets, shiny wood coat rack housing a long black robe, and a pipe collection held in a polished wood stand. Jackson sniffed in the room's aromatic pipe tobacco smell; a nice scent compared to his father's leftover cigarette-reek that lingered in their furniture. His finger wedged between his shirt collar and sweaty neck. On this Tuesday afternoon his mother made her sons deck out in their Sunday finest of white shirts, bow ties, and slacks. She looked pretty in her beige church dress and nylons.

On the other side of the room, Jackson's uncles Ernie and Eddie Kingman scowled in their direction. Sheriff Quinn and Doctor Mann sat between the feuding families with their hats in their hands. Why had Judge Lane asked the county sheriff and doctor to attend? Maybe the judge was expecting trouble.

With a pipe wedged between his teeth, Judge Lane used a forefinger to slide across paragraphs he was reviewing. Jackson held back a smile. His teacher would scold the judge if he was sitting in her classroom for using a finger as a reading aid. Wouldn't that be something; a lady teacher lecturing a grey-haired old man who was powerful enough to send a criminal to "Old Sparky."

"I realize it's a bit crowded in here," the judge said in a heavy West Virginian accent. "Sorry for the inconvenience. You're probably wondering why I called this meeting today. Every so often the district attorney asks me to speak to the individuals involved in cases before it goes to a grand jury - a preliminary hearing if you will."

The judge's chambers gave Jackson goose bumps. His legs were shaking. Jim stared at his shiny brown oxfords, his way of being invisible. To be in a room with these officials would have been an honor to brag about, but it could be the worst day in Jackson's life if his mother was sent to jail for murder.

"Before we proceed," the judge said, scanning seven faces, "for those of you who do not know me by reputation, I will not tolerate any form of perjury, large or small, in my courtroom or chambers. If you dare fabricate the truth - lie - you will pay the consequences. This rule would also apply to Mrs. Kingman's court ordered attorney had she not waived her right to have him be present here today. Is this understood by all?"

Everyone nodded or said yes except Jim.

"On my left we have Ernest and Edwin Kingman," the judge said. "Which one is which?"

"I'm Ernest Kingman," the taller uncle said, throwing a thumb at his brother. "This here bearded fella is Edwin."

"Everyone calls me Eddie, your judgeship."

For the first time, Jackson realized how much all three brothers looked alike; thin with brown hair and eyes. They sounded similar, with distinctive deep pleasing voices. The only difference, his father had a natural ability to capture and keep someone's attention. People lost interest in his uncles after a few words. His mother once told him he inherited the Kingman features, voice, and his father's gift of gab. Jackson clenched his jaw, hoping his father didn't pass along any of his bad traits.

"The Kingman brothers filed a petition to have a grand jury try Ellie Kingman for the murder of their brother Emmett Kingman." The judge ran a finger twice over words in his file. "In your statement it says you have undeniable evidence Ellie Kingman planned to kill her husband Emmett. Perhaps it would be in the best interests of this session if you would verbally share your irrefutable proof the murder of your brother Emmett was premeditated; meaning planned in advance and carried out willfully by his wife Ellie."

The two uncles whispered back and forth. Uncle Eddie scratched his beard and shrugged his shoulders. Jackson wished he had the ability to read lips.

"We don't quite understand what you mean, judge." Uncle Ernie rose to his feet. "But Ellie meant to kill our brother in cold blood. That much we know for sure."

"Mrs. Kingman gave her statement to the responding deputy sheriff. She admitted shooting her husband with a shotgun. That fact isn't in question here." The judge puffed out smoke. "The issue is why she pulled the trigger. The two of you seem to have information questioning her version of why the shooting took place. Were either of you a witness to the shooting?"

Jackson leaned forward. His uncles lied all the time just like his father - the reason he walked away with so many door-to-door vacuum cleaner sales. The judge said there wouldn't be any lying. Were his uncle's dumb enough to say they saw his mother shoot his father?

"Nah, we didn't see Ellie gun down Emmett," Uncle Eddie said. "We didn't have to. Sure as shit... ah sugar, we knew she'd kill him someday - just a matter of when. And we got proof she wanted to kill Emmett."

"Your statement today could be pertinent to the outcome of this case." The judge closed one eye. "How did you come by this knowledge?"

"Emmett told us hundreds of times Ellie hated him," Uncle Ernie said. "He warned us she'd shoot him when he had his guard down. Ever since they had to get married, our brother feared for his life for obvious reasons. The proof is in the shootin.'"

"Do you have Emmett's account in writing he feared for his life?" Judge Lane penciled notes while he asked the question.

"Well, no your honor," Uncle Ernie said. "None of us read or write too good. Emmett, he was the oldest, got farther in school than me and Eddie, but we don't diary our talks. But it's the truth, judge, so help me God. She wanted Emmett dead."

Jackson's stomach burned. He ground the heel of his shoe into the floor. His uncles were lying. It was the other way around; his mother feared his father. She was cautious about not setting off his hair-trigger temper. Earlier, the judge promised not to let them get away with lying. If a twelve year old could recognize a lie, why couldn't the judge?

"Is there anyone else you know of who could corroborate Emmett's fear he related to you and your brother?" the judge asked. "For example, did either of you or your brother Emmett ever report these suspicions to the law or anyone else?"

"In all honesty, it was family business, Judge. So me and Ernest didn't say nothin' to nobody. Maybe Emmett did. He was real scared." Uncle Eddie pointed at Jackson's mother. "That woman's evil. She'd been planning to shoot our brother for a long time."

"Ernest," the judge said, "you and Edwin have repeatedly stated today your brother Emmett was convinced his wife would shoot him. How come he wasn't afraid she would poison him? Or suffocate him in his sleep. Or impale him with a knife."

"Emmett always told us she'd shoot him," Uncle Ernie said. "His exact words. Makes sense. Everybody's got guns in these parts and knows how to use 'em. Hell, to my know-how, there ain't no easier way to get the deed done." He frowned at Jackson's mother. "I don't mind tellin' you, judge, Eddie and me don't feel safe as long as that woman's free to walk the streets of West Virginia."

The judge relit his pipe, sucking on the end until clouds of smoke blew out. With his left hand he wrote more notes, removed the pipe from his mouth, and asked if they had anything else to add. The two uncles shook their heads.

"Mrs. Kingman," the judge said. "I have your sworn statement saying your husband was drunk, shot a hole in the kitchen stove, and wanted to take his son Jackson out squirrel hunting. It says here you warned your husband he was in no condition to go hunting. When he didn't heed your warning, you shot him with a shotgun to protect your son. Is there anything you want to add or delete from this statement?"

Jackson's mother played with an earring. She glanced at Jackson, then back at the judge.

"I don't want to change anything, judge. It happened the way I said."

Jackson stared at his mother, willing her to fight for herself the same way she fought to save him. If she was sent to jail, what would happen to him and Jim? Would the court order them to live with their uncles? Another sharp pain pierced the walls of his stomach. He'd take Jim and run away before he'd let his uncles do parenting.

"Is there anything you want to say, doc?" The judge pointed his pipe at the doctor.

"Absolutely." The doctor glanced at Jackson's mother. "I've been Ellie Kingman's physician for fourteen years. She is a fine woman and a fine mother. She loves them two boys to death. On three occasions, Ellie came to my office battered. The last time I treated her was when she came home from a trip to Mexico City with her husband. She was beaten up pretty bad. Contusions and cuts on her arms, chest, and stomach. And her left wrist was severely sprained."

"Did Mrs. Kingman say her husband beat her? Or wanted her husband dead?"

"No, Judge. As you know, I've been doctoring for a long time. Treated a number of patient wife beatings. Rarely does a wife say her husband beats on her. Or their kids." The doctor wiped a hand over his mouth. "I think it's because the wives are afraid their husbands will retaliate and rough the family up even more severely."

"Thank you, doc," the judge said. "Mrs. Kingman, did your husband beat you?"

She peered at her brother-in-laws again. "No, your honor."

"But Mom," Jackson blurted out. "That's not—"

Jackson's mother gave him a stern look along with a quick knee jab to his thigh. The judge had told them not to lie. Did she think the uncles would beat on him and Jim if she squealed on their brother?

"You see, judge." Uncle Eddie jumped up. "That quack don't know what he's talkin' about. Emmett would never beat up no woman."

"You had a chance to speak," the judge said. "Now sit down and be quiet."

Jackson wouldn't show his uncles the fear inside of him. He glared back at them the same way they eyed his mother. How could he help her when she wouldn't help herself?

The judge shifted his view to the Sheriff. "Do you have something to say, Charlie?"

"Sure do, judge," the broad shouldered sheriff said. "Ernie and Eddie Kingman have a high opinion of their late brother Emmett. So do I, as a matter of fact."

Jackson's stomach rumbled loud enough for everyone to hear. The sheriff might as well have put steel handcuffs on his mother's wrists and an iron ball around her ankles. Did the uncles give the sheriff money to lie to the judge?

"As I was saying, I take my hat off to Emmett Kingman. He was one cagey hombre. I've never met a man who could get himself in and out of more scrapes with the law than Emmett and not have his profile picture hanging on our post office wall." The sheriff rested a palm on the butt of his holstered gun. "Is he a wife beater? Only Ellie and her boys can answer that question. I will tell you Emmett Kingman was well known in these parts by sheriffs and deputies for public drunkenness, petty theft, fighting, fraud, disturbing the peace, reckless driving, and running over a man with his car. I know Ellie Kingman. Like doc said, she's a fine woman. If Ellie used a shotgun on Emmett, she had a darn good reason to do so. Protecting her sons is a darn good reason in my book."

"Thank you, sheriff." Judge Lane closed his file. "Mrs. Kingman, do you recall what I said about telling the truth in my chambers?"

"Yes I do, judge." She straightened her shoulders.

The judge emptied his pipe bowl into an ashtray. His chair squeaked when he put the pipe in the only vacant slot in the pipe stand. He turned to face his audience.

"Jackson," the judge announced, with a serious expression.

Jackson twitched when his name was called. "Ye...Yes sir."

"Sorry to bring you and your brother into this. Is there anything you want to say, son?"

"What the hell do you think the kid's going say, judge?" Uncle Eddie shouted. "He ain't gonna to say nothin' against his ma."

"One more outburst from you, Edwin Kingman, and I will hold you and your brother in contempt." The judge nodded to Jackson. "Go ahead, son."

Jackson put a hand on his stomach. He didn't know what to say. If he told Judge Lane the truth, his mother would go to jail for lying. Then again, if he didn't tell the truth, his mother would probably go to jail for murder.

"My mother was right, Judge. My father was drunk. He wanted me to get up out of bed to go hunting with him on a school day. Mom got a shotgun off the wall and ordered him to stop. She didn't want me getting hurt because of the condition he was in, especially after shooting up the kitchen stove."

"Thank you for verifying your mother's statement, Jackson." The judge sighed.

"There's more, Judge." Jackson stood. "My mother told my father if he took one more step towards our bedroom door, she would shoot him."

"Yes, we are aware of that, Jackson. If there's nothing—"

"My father laughed when my mother told him not to take another step," Jackson said. "Then he told my mother, 'You ain't never pulled a trigger in your life, Ellie. You don't have the grits to shoot me or anything else.' Then he cussed her."

"Had you ever seen your mother shoot a gun before, Jackson?"

"Never. She hates guns 'cause they stink and make too much noise."

"Anything else, son?" The judge's cold eyes focused on the Kingman brothers.

"My mom didn't say the truth about the beatings because she was afraid our uncles will beat on Jim and me the same way our father did. She's always looking out for us, even if it hurts her. Judge, isn't there a straining thing to keep them away from us?"

"You mean a restraining order." The judge chuckled. "Good idea, Jackson. You're going to be one heck of a litigator someday, but I'll do you one better." He waved the file at the brothers. "I'm fining both of you one hundred dollars for lying in my chambers. Your answers to my next two questions could make the difference between jail time and a prison term. Have either one of you ever seen Ellie Kingman with a gun in her hands?"

Both brothers looked at each other. "No, your honor."

"Did your brother Emmett ever say to you he feared his wife would shoot him?"

"Not exactly in them words, judge," Uncle Ernest said. "But Emmett really did say she hated him."

"Sheriff Quinn, arrest these two for contempt of court," Judge Lane ordered.

"My pleasure, judge." The sheriff pulled handcuffs from his belt.

Judge Lane repacked his pipe with tobacco. Jackson's mom was explaining something to Jim. Jackson moved into the aisle. Uncle Eddy turned and sneered at Jackson when a handcuff snapped closed on his wrist.

"Your big mouth got us in this mess, boy," Uncle Eddy growled in a low tone. "You may be kin, but someday me and Ernie are gonna to getcha like your ma got our brother."

Jackson didn't breathe until the sheriff led the cuffed uncles through the door. Telling his mom what Uncle Eddy had said would only make her worry more. Even though the uncles lied to the judge, this time Jackson knew his Uncle Eddy was telling the truth.

"Mrs. Kingman," Judge Lane said, puffing out a stream of smoke. "I don't condone taking the law into one's own hands. But I do believe you did so in the best interest of your sons to protect them. This case will not go to the grand jury." The judge rose. "However, I highly recommend you and the boys move away from this state as soon as possible. If you don't, the Kingman name will forever follow you like a Cajun curse."

CHAPTER THREE

Jackson squatted behind home plate and gave Wesley, his new best friend, a good warm-up pitch target. His voice squeaked encouragement to his battery mate, one of the many body changes Jackson was experiencing at twelve years old. He couldn't remember the name of the first baseman rolling ground balls to the other infielders, but spring heat had replaced a frosty winter and baseball season was in full bloom.

After attending nine different primary schools by the seventh grade, being the new kid in the classroom or on a team wasn't a challenge for Jackson. He had a natural talent to make friends even in hostile environments. With a father like Emmett Kingman, Jackson was used to moving from one city or county to another in a moment's notice. If his father wasn't searching for another job or sales territory, he was avoiding the law. One rumor had his father leaving town overnight to hide out in a neighboring city after running over and killing a Negro man with his car.

Jackson fired the baseball back to Wesley. He loved being a catcher. The position gave him prestige. He could control a game and handle each pitch instead of standing around. Better yet, he could hide behind a metal mask for half the game.

Jackson removed his bloated catcher's mitt and shook out dirt. He recalled a time when the man who owned the feed store watched Jackson catch both ends of a double-header. The owner made a point of telling his mother what a good player Jackson was. She had rubbed Jackson's crew cut and smiled. He didn't feel worthy of the praise, but the owner's words made his mother happy.

The stands behind each dugout were filled with parents and kids. Jackson couldn't spot the feed store owner in the crowd. If the man was in attendance, he'd probably be saying awful things about Jackson and the Kingman family behind their backs like everyone else in these parts. The notorious Ellie Kingman and her boys had become an ongoing story for newspapers, radio, and rumormongers. One piece of gossip had his mother shooting at a deputy. Another spreading tale had his mother catching his father with another woman. Last week Jackson heard someone say his mom shot his dad for the insurance money; a theory that made him laugh. If there had been insurance money, they wouldn't have to mooch off of his grandmother. Grandma Adams, his mother's maiden name and his middle name, didn't want them living with her anymore than they wanted to be there.

Jackson threw a strike to second base after receiving Wesley's last warm-up pitch. Pete Long stepped into the batter's box. Tall, husky, and a city kid, Pete was the best hitter in the league. He smoothed loose dirt with his spikes towards the back of the box before kicking most of the soil onto Jackson's worn Keds.

"I'm only helping you out, Kingman." Pete looked down at Jackson. "Don't all you country boys who ride the school bus play in the dirt?"

Jackson ignored Pete. His mother had told Jackson to turn a deaf ear to all the cruel words fired at him and his brother Jim from teasing kids and their annoying parents. Even if he had a deaf ear, the other ear would hear plenty.

He gave a forefinger signal to throw a fastball, the only decent pitch Wesley had. Wesley stopped in the middle of his windup when Jackson placed the target four inches off the plate outside. Jackson punched the pocket of his mitt to reinforce the call. Wesley shrugged his shoulders, went back into his windup, and hit the target perfectly.

"Ball," the umpire-father yelled from behind the pitcher's mound. Jackson nodded his approval and threw the ball back to Wesley. He gave the same sign and target. Same result. If bucketmouth Pete Long was going to get a hit today, he would need a longer bat. Or he would be called out for stepping on or across the plate when he swung his bat.

"I was wrong, Kingman." Pete leaned on his bat as if it was a walking cane. "You don't need a school bus. Your murdering mother can drop you off in a paddy wagon on the way to the slammer where she belongs."

Jackson could taste his building fury. Pete was four inches taller and at least twenty pounds heavier. Jackson had never been in a fight in his life, afraid his mother wouldn't approve. Afraid his father would have called him a sissy if he lost. Afraid of what he might do to the other person if he unleashed his temper.

Pete grunted out a laugh, stepped out of the batter's box, and took a mighty practice swing so close to Jackson's head he felt the breeze. Pete changed his batting stance by planting the tips of his spikes on the inner white chalked line. His elbows hung over the middle of the plate. If they were playing football, Pete would have been whistled offside.

Jackson flipped his middle finger between his legs and angled the finger in Pete's direction. Wesley nodded. Jackson gave another outside target just in case Pete was sneaking a quick look. Wesley double pumped a windup to get more velocity. As soon as the ball left Wesley's hand, it zeroed in on Pete's temple. Pete's hat and bat went flying as the ball whizzed by his head and went to the back-stop. He dropped to the dirt as if there were no bones left in his body. Alarmed shrieks came from the stands as Jackson retrieved the ball. Pete was out of breath when he opened his eyes and realized he wasn't hurt. The back of his uniform was covered with dirt and chalk. Pete glared his hate first at Wesley, then at Jackson. The catcher's mask didn't hide Jackson's gloating grin.

"The fruit from the Kingman family tree looks the same," Pete spit out. "Dirty on the outside and rotten on the inside like your ma."

"Watch out, Pete. The ball might not miss your big head this time. Maybe you shouldn't crowd the plate. My pitcher's a bit wild today."

"Listen good, pipsqueak." Pete reached for his hat. "If one more pitch comes near me, I'm going to drag the infield with your sorry ass."

Jackson tackled Pete. Lying on top, Jackson pounded the bully's face with his metal catcher's mask over and over again. Each smash felt better than the other. Pete's face was a bloody mess by the time several hands pulled Jackson off of him.

Jackson straddled home plate. Players and coaches from both teams huddled in front of their respective dugouts. Pete's dad put a fist in Jackson's face, growled like a mountain lion, and led his sobbing son to the dugout while holding a towel over his pulpy mug.

From the stands, parents screamed at Jackson as if he was vermin. Maybe he was. The terrible temper hidden inside of him had been set free, no doubt a trait inherited from his father. If they hadn't stopped the beating, he might have pounded Pete to death in front of dozens of witnesses. The authorities would probably put his soon-to-be thirteen year old fanny in jail for life based on his mother's reputation. He had won the battle with Pete, but lost the war. He hated losing. Next time, he would figure out a way to win both.

Jackson left the chest protector, shin guards, and catcher's mask piled on home plate. The black protective bar on the mask was two-toned in red. He wiped sweat from his face and realized the back of his hand was spotted with Pete's sticky blood.

Jackson grabbed his catcher's mitt and lit out in the direction of his grandmother's house, serenaded by boos and shouts. They had lived with his grandma for less than a month. Good thing his mother saved all the packing boxes. The Kingman family would need to find another city to live in. Once again, he had failed his mother.

CHAPTER FOUR

A blistering winter wind shook the small rental house, causing the lights to flicker. Jackson marked the page of the library book he had been reading and scooted his kitchen chair an inch closer to the potbelly stove. Mickey, a miniature brown and white mutt who adopted the family when they moved in three months ago, settled in on the linoleum floor by his slippers. His tireless mother had found another county for the Kingman family to live in after his fight on the ball field with Pete Long.

1961's chart-topping song, "Tossin' and Turnin'" by Bobby Lewis sounded from radio station KGR. Baseball's off season allowed Jackson to catch up on the latest tunes. If this was a summer night, he would abandon music for stations that carried Cincinnati Redlegs and Atlanta Crackers baseball games.

Warm and toasty, he went to the sink to wash his hands. Mickey stayed by the stove's heat. Back at his chair, he opened one of the cigar boxes on the table next to a stack of newly acquired baseball cards. The box, lined with his mother's aluminum foil, contained his most prized possessions wrapped in wax paper envelopes; baseball cards collected from American Tobacco, Cracker Jack, Bowman, Leaf Candy, Post Toasties, Fleer, and Topps. He didn't use rubber bands because they indented the sides.

Only three baseball card companies were still in business. Each cigar box represented a different category: players inducted into the hall of fame like Honus Wagnor, Babe Ruth, and Ty Cobb; players Jackson considered future hall of famers; and popular player cards used for trading with other kids not as savvy as Jackson.

He straightened the cards he had traded for. Statistics and personal information on the front and back of each card were etched in his memory. Money was scarce in the Kingman household since his father's death. Jackson couldn't buy new cards. Instead, he acquired coveted players by bartering with classmates and kids in the neighborhood and at school. To clinch a deal, he would often throw in stale rectangles of pink bubblegum.

His eyes watered after a yawn. Someday he would be rich enough to buy every baseball card ever printed and a house for his mother so she would never have to move again. If he didn't make it to the big leagues, he would own a business involved in making deals. People who owned businesses had money. Power of money gave them a respectful status.

The potbelly stove hummed and crackled. How long would it be before they had to pack up and move to another city or county? He was sure Grandma Adams was giving his mother a lending hand, but it couldn't have been a huge sum of money since his grandmother didn't have much to spare.

Jim's schoolbooks were on the far end of the kitchen table. He was asleep in their bedroom. Without a father, even a mean boozer of a father who never had a kind word for his sons or wife, Jackson felt pressure to help raise Jim. The brothers were three years apart, but the gap in their personalities widened each day. Jim was shy, excelled in academics, and wasn't much of an athlete. Jackson got by without doing much homework, loved sports, blended in socially, and could talk his way out of most anything.

A spelling championship certificate of honor scotch taped to the refrigerator caught Jackson's eye. He loved to compete. He darn well wasn't going to let a snooty city kid win the seventh grade spelling championship. He never did receive the award at the school's assembly because his family had to move away in a hurry. The certificate came in the mail several weeks later. The award meant more to his mother than to him. His real reward was beating the words out of the city kid.

He arched his elbows on the table, closed his stinging eyes, and laid his head on his forearms. His breathing deepened. Gentle hands massaged his shoulders making his eyelids lift.

"Did you do your homework, Jackson?" His mother sat down next to him. "All of it?"

"Most of it, Mom. I can wing the rest."

"Are those new baseball cards?"

"I traded with a kid at school."

"Who got the better of the trade?"

"I swapped the Cincinnati Redleg players he wanted," Jackson said, with a sly grin, "for a bunch of great players from the twenties and thirties that are hard to find."

"You're quite a salesman - like your father, only honest. I've been thinking of our chitchat from the other night. You opened my eyes about how our moving from one West Virginia city to another is getting us nowhere. It's time we settled down in one place."

"Are you saying someone is after us again? We're running out of counties to live in."

"Maybe counties, but not states, dear. Do you remember I mentioned we had an aunt in Reno, Nevada? Aunt Bessie really isn't an aunt. She's your grandmother's good friend."

"Sure. I read up on Reno at the library. It's called the biggest little city in the world. They even have a minor league baseball team called the Silver Sox. And mines full of silver."

"After our talk, I called Aunt Bessie. She will put the three of us up for awhile until we get back on our feet. You're not old enough to realize there aren't very many good jobs for young men around here, especially with a tainted name. And I can't find a decent job 'cause folks think I'm gonna shoot them. You and Jim are smart. I could never afford to send either one of you to college. After high school, most likely you boys would be forced to work the coal mines or join the military." His mom ran a hand over his crew cut. "Moving to Reno can give us a chance for a normal life."

Jackson pondered the idea of a "normal life," whatever that might be. The Kingman family had worn out their welcome in West Virginia. Living in Nevada, or any other state, had to be better. With no history to haunt them, maybe he could stop fretting about the nasty things people spit out about his family. He was more than willing to go to Reno, but something his mother had said didn't set well with him.

"Promise me two things, Mom, and I will even talk Jim into liking Reno," he said. "Is there a baseball league for boys my age?"

"Aunt Bessie said they have baseball programs for all ages. What's the second thing?"

Jackson bobbed his head and pointed under the table. "There are four of us."

"We can hardly afford..." she reached down to give Mickey a loving pat on the head. "Okay, Jackson. We'll take the dog along."

Jackson smiled and carefully placed the new baseball cards into a cigar box. His mother probably would have thrown in a new catcher's mitt to get his blessings. His stomach growled. On the flip side, what if his knack for making friends and deals didn't work in Nevada? He was a good catcher, but not an all star. What if he wasn't good enough to make the team? What if...

"I detect wrinkles of fear on your face, Jackson. I've only been out of West Virginia twice in my life. Moving away for good scares the bejeebers out of me too, but it's for our own good. There's so much to do before we go. The station wagon needs to get checked out. We have to sell our furniture. And I need to find a person who will share the driving with me. I was talking to a young fella in his teens or early twenties who works at a gas station and wants to get out of West Virginia in the worst way. His name is Dalton Peppers. Maybe he'd want to go to Reno with us. It won't hurt to have another grownup - someone who could be a big brother to you and Jim. Maybe he would even chip in with gas money."

Jackson tied string around the cigar box. A big brother? He had never considered what it would be like to have an older brother. Someone, other than his mother, who could explain certain facts to him. The name Dalton Peppers rang a familiar bell. Jackson had heard or seen that name before, but he couldn't remember where.

CHAPTER FIVE

The station wagon bounced twice, waking Jackson from his backseat nap. An afternoon sun made him squint and blink. "Hit the Road Jack," Ray Charles' current hit song was playing on the radio. Where the heck where they? Each state highway looked pretty much the same as the other.

A front tire hit another road rut. They passed a sign "Welcome to Kansas - the Sunflower State" - answering his question. He had slept through most of Missouri.

Mickey's furry body snuggled between the brothers. Jim was reading an old *Reader's Digest*. Jackson's mother dozed with her head against a pillow braced on the passenger side window while Dalton Peppers manned the steering wheel with his left hand. His free hand combed through short, light-brown hair. Jackson picked at a finger cuticle. Why couldn't he remember where he had seen or heard Dalton's name?

Before the family departed West Virginia, Jackson met Dalton for the first time at a garage where he worked as a junior mechanic. Dalton was several inches taller than Jackson and stocky. He seemed nice enough; quiet, polite, and sociable in a shy way. He was only a year out of high school, but Jackson's mother thought they would be better protected traveling cross country with a young man on board. Dalton told them he had a job offer from an uncle who owned an auto repair garage near Sacramento, California.

Dalton flipped down the visor, gazed at Jackson in the rear-view mirror, and smiled.

Jackson looked away. Dalton had blushed when Jackson's mother asked if he was leaving a bunch of girlfriends behind. Did she really believe Dalton was handsome? A major pimple outbreak decorated both of his cheeks and forehead; as if a bird had been pecking on his face. And he had weird eyes that weren't the same color. One was blue and the other was brown.

Jackson yawned and stretched his arms. A series of road signs, his mother called them billboards, lined both sides of the highway as if they grew straight from the ground. One billboard advertised a Mobil gas station two miles ahead giving away S&H Green Stamps with a fill up. Another board promoted a state fair. They zoomed past a sign advertising Rusty's Burger Shack - Take The Next Exit. Most of the wood structures were two-sided and came in different heights and sizes. Some even had lights for night viewing.

Jackson's nose inched close enough to the window to fog up a portion. He was tempted to ask Dalton to pull over to the side of the road so he could touch and examine the structures. A man in grey overalls stood high up on a ledge attached to one of the billboards by rope painting a cowboy's face that had a cigarette dangling from his lips. From the highway, the artwork looked like a large magazine ad. Was the painter an actual artist? Or maybe it was similar to a paint-by-number kit grandma labored on.

The station wagon passed a vacant billboard with ADVERTISE HERE and a phone number painted in big black letters on a yellow background. A flood of questions popped into Jackson's head. Could anyone advertise on a billboard? How much did it cost? Who owned the billboards? How often did they change the message?

Mickey whimpered the way dogs do when they are dreaming. Jackson gave him a soft nudge. A billboard across the road pictured Electrolux Vacuum Cleaners. His father could have made a ton of door sales in this area from that sign alone. Every time his father had a good day selling vacuum cleaners, he celebrated with a bottle of whiskey. The more he drank the meaner he got. Things were even more difficult for his mom since his dad died, but she appeared to be a whole lot happier with him gone.

Jackson removed tradable baseball cards from his shirt pocket. He envisioned himself on a billboard holding up a handful of his most valuable cards: JACKSON KINGMAN, BASEBALL CARD KING, HAVE CARDS - WILL TRADE...

POP! A rhythmic *thump, thump, thump,* followed. Dalton fought to control the steering wheel. Jim shrieked and dropped his *Reader's Digest.* A truck horn blared from behind. The station wagon front snaked from one side of the road to the other. Jackson prevented

Mickey from falling onto the floorboard with one hand while he grabbed the back of the front bench seat with the other hand, as if they were on a county fair amusement ride. His mother took a quick tight-lipped glance at her sons.

Dalton had both hands on the steering wheel. He managed to guide the car off the highway and onto the dirt roadside until it limped to a stop. A dirt dust storm flew up around the front and sides of the station wagon. One by one they filed from the car, except for Jim who was sucking his thumb. Mickey rushed to a dry bush and lifted his leg. In a calm voice his mother urged Jim to join them, with no luck.

"Oh my God, Dalton," she gushed, clutching his arm. "You were wonderful. I don't know what would have happened if I had been driving? You saved our lives."

Dalton's face colored to a brighter shade of red. "It was only a blowout, Mrs. Kingman."

"I assume you know how to change a flat tire since you're a mechanic?" she said.

"Yes, ma'am." Dalton pointed at the spare tire attached to the tailgate. "I changed plenty of tires at the gas station. Don't suppose you know where the jack is located?"

"The jack? I think it's behind the tire."

"Don't worry, Mrs. Kingman." Dalton twisted a metal cap holding the tire. "I'll find it."

A semi-truck pulled up behind the station wagon. With the motor idling, a driver wearing a sweat stained t-shirt, jeans, green military hat, and boots climbed down from the cab and approached Jackson's mother as Dalton removed the spare tire.

"Saw the tire blow." The driver adjusted his crusty cap and nodded to Dalton. "Your boy here did some fancy driving. If you need any assistance, ma'am, we truckers always try to aid other drivers, especially pretty moms with kin."

"Thank you," she said. "But I think we're in good hands. It was nice of you to stop."

Jackson picked up Mickey. The truck driver tipped his hat to his mother and retraced his long stride foot tracks back to the truck.

Jackson had heard other men call his mother pretty. Did Dalton agree to come along because his pretty mother paid attention to him and West Virginia girls didn't?

"Jackson, we are going to celebrate Dalton's heroic feat of saving us from God knows what by staying in a motel tonight." She gave Mickey a couple of head pats. "Pay attention to what Dalton is doing. You can learn a lot from that young man."

With the jack and tire iron in hand, Dalton turned and smiled.

* * * * *

Jackson propped the pillow against the twin bed headboard as his mother stared into the motel room's mirror above the dresser to apply lipstick. The funny faces she made amused him. She was wearing the same dress and nylons she wore in Judge Lane's chambers. Jim stood next to her. She replaced the lipstick top back onto the tube, combed Jim's hair with a hand, and straightened his bowtie.

The other twin bed his mother had slept in was straightened up for the maid, which made sense only to his mother. Dalton had his knees planted into the worn motel carpet while he rolled up his sleeping bag. He didn't mind sleeping on the floor.

"Jackson," she gazed at his image in the mirror, "there's still time to change your mind. Are you sure you won't go to church with Jim and me?"

"I'm sure, Mom."

"The only reason I'm allowing you to skip church this Sunday morning is because Dalton is with us and he doesn't attend services. Otherwise, there is no way I would let you stay in a motel room alone." She opened her purse and placed a fifty cent piece on the dresser. "I remember seeing a donut shop down the block in case you boys get hungry. Bring back a glazed donut for your brother Jim and change."

"Thanks, Mrs. Kingman." Dalton tied a cord around the sleeping bag. "Sugar and chocolate donuts are my breakfast of champions next to Wheaties."

"We'll be back in a couple of hours." She turned around before opening the door. "Jackson, you mind Dalton, now."

"Yes, ma'am."

Dalton moved to the window and pinched back the curtain. The station wagon engine rattled to a start and backed away. He stayed at the window for awhile until the curtain slipped from his fingers. He went to Jackson's bed and shook it with both hands.

"Get up, lazybones," Dalton said. "I need to show you a thing or two."

"I'm comfortable." Jackson's pajama clad legs performed a butterfly swim move under the covers, shifting Mickey on top. "Sleeping in the car is crampy. I doubt my mom will pay for another motel. Wish I was more like my brother. He can nod off anywhere."

"Remember, your ma told you I was in charge. Come on, we don't got much time."

Jackson rubbed sleep from his eyes and threw back the covers. His mother usually forced him to get up out of bed. Having someone else do it didn't feel quite right. His bare feet hit the scratchy rug as he rubbed the pajama top sleeves with both hands.

"Your ma said you all are going to Nevada. Where in Nevada?"

"Reno."

"How do you feel about going to a new school? That can be rough on a kid your age."

"We've moved around West Virginia so much I'm used to being the new kid."

"You seem like a smart guy. Do you get good grades?"

"They're okay. My brother Jim is a real good student."

"What's your favorite thing to do in the whole world?" Dalton asked.

"Play baseball."

"Too much standing around for me." Dalton opened a suitcase. "You pretty good?"

"I guess. I'm always first string, probably because I'm a catcher. Most kids shy away from catching because you get nicked up all the time. I think it's the best position of all."

"Your ma is real nice. And pretty too."

Jackson hitched his shoulders.

"You got a girlfriend?" Dalton asked.

"Nah." Every time Jackson got cozy with a girl, the family had to skedaddle out of town.

Jackson could see the back of Dalton through the dresser mirror. Dalton hardly talked when Jim and his mother were around. Why was he so talkative all of a sudden?

"I was wondering." Dalton hefted a green duffle bag secured at the top with a heavy looking metal padlock onto the bed next to his suitcase. "What do you keep in them cigar boxes? Must be somethin' really valuable like rare coins or gold."

"Better." Jackson pointed to the cigar boxes piled on the nightstand. "My baseball cards."

"Everyone has baseball cards. What's so special about yours?"

"Bet I have the best collection in West Virginia. I wouldn't sell it for a million bucks."

"Those cards are really important to you." Dalton produced an exaggerated whistle. "Can I see them?"

"No!" Jackson studied the lumpy green bag. "What's in your duffle bag?"

"Mementos I've collected." Dalton rubbed fingers over the rough surface. "And it will soon get heavier. You know your ma asked me to teach you some things."

"What kind of things?"

"Nature like things that should come natural, but don't unless introduced proper like." Dalton said. "I'm gonna take a shower. You should join me."

Dalton peeled off his t-shirt to expose a muscled chest and a chain with a gold key. He pulled down grey sweat pants, exposing a large bulge behind his underwear.

"I took a shower last night." Jackson's hands formed into fists. "I don't need one."

Dalton's eyes slit into a menacing stare as he stepped towards Jackson. Jackson reared his fist back and fired it at Dalton's chin. Dalton caught the punch with one hand before the blow landed.

"I asked you nicely," Dalton spit out. "Now I'm not asking. You either take a shower with me or I'll kill your ma and brother when they come back from church."

* * * * *

Jackson stood by the nightstand twisting the radio dial when his mother and Jim came back from church. He was fully dressed, but felt naked. The radio's needle had moved from one end to the other without his finding a static-free station.

"Where's Dalton?" His mother removed her coat.

"He took the four bits from the dresser and headed for the donut shop."

"Why didn't you go with him?"

"He said to wait here. You told me I had to mind him."

"How long ago did he leave?"

"Half an hour - maybe more."

"You're as white as Casper the Ghost." She put the back of her hand on his forehead and searched the room with her eyes. "You don't have a fever. Where are Dalton's bags?"

"He took them with him, Mom. Dalton's not coming back."

"You promised me a glazed donut," Jim said in a whiny voice.

"I'll get you a donut, Jim," she said. "At least he didn't take anything else."

Jackson couldn't hold back his tears. "He stole my baseball card collection."

"What!" She wrapped her arms around him. "I'm so sorry, sweetheart. It's all my fault. How could I have misjudged him like that?"

Jackson struggled to catch his breath. He was too ashamed to tell her about being brutally abused in the shower. The act had made him remember where he had seen Dalton's name. It was written on a public bathroom wall in ink next to a drawn penis.

Jackson hated Dalton like God hated sin.

CHAPTER SIX

Downtown Reno sidewalks were busy with tourists - many of them casino gamblers - taking in the sights, sounds, and smells of the biggest little city in the world. The only building Jackson had any interest in was the new downtown Reno library; his home away from Aunt Bessie's house since the Kingman family arrived six months earlier.

Jackson scurried up the cement steps and threw open the heavy entrance door. The Reno library was massive compared to the libraries he frequented in West Virginia. He placed the books he had previously checked out on the drop-off counter and went directly to the "Ernest Hemingway section." He removed from the shelf *A Farewell to Arms* and *The Old Man and the Sea.*

Mrs. Gray, the white-haired librarian, smiled when he handed her his library card and books to be checked out. She was heavy and if possible even older than Aunt Bessie who had dark brown hair. A necklace watch dangled over her enormous bosom. Jackson shied away from examining the watch face. She was nice, always complimenting him on something.

"I think you are our best customer, Jackson." She flipped over the cover and stamped the date in blue ink. "We don't have many avid readers your age. When you are done with Hemingway, I have other authors I'm sure you will enjoy reading."

"Thank you, ma'am. I have more time to read when it's not baseball season."

"A reader and a ballplayer. What a great combination." She stamped the second book. "What part of West Virginia are you from?"

"How did you know I came from West Virginia?"

"From your accent."

"Oh." Jackson rolled his eyes as he studied his sneakers.

"What's the matter, Jackson? Do your classmates tease you because of the way you talk?"

Jackson nodded. The friendly librarian had nailed his biggest problem since they arrived in Reno. He stood out like a left-hand throwing catcher. He tried to mimic the way his fellow students spoke, but the words came out different, hindering a knack he had for winning over new people right from the start. One kid kept calling him Vic the Hick.

"What I don't get is how you knew I was from West Virginia," he said.

"I started working at the library after my husband passed away. For most of my life I was a speech therapist. I have a good ear for territorial accents. You see, Jackson, I was born and raised in Boston, Massachusetts. The reason I went into speech therapy is because I had a thick Boston accent; I pahked my cah at Hahvuhd yahd."

Jackson giggled at her unusual accent.

"Countless people reacted the same way as you did when I spoke," she said. "It really, really bothered me."

"But you don't have an accent now."

"Thank you for noticing. I lost my accent after my parents sent me to a speech therapist."

"My mom can't even afford a place to live let alone a speech teacher," Jackson said in a deflated tone.

"How hard are you willing to work at ridding your tiny West Virginia accent?"

"Real hard, ma'am. But I don't know how."

"Jackson, I'm willing to volunteer my time to teach you, with your mother's permission, of course. We can set up a schedule based on my library hours and your school program."

Wow. How lucky could he be after coming from a place where friends and strangers were constantly criticizing him and his family or avoiding to lend a helping hand. Then again, why would Mrs. Gray offer to do such a nice thing for someone she hardly knew?

Mrs. Gray slid the books across the counter and touched Jackson's hand before he could pick them up.

"By the doubt registered on your face, you're wondering why I would go out of my way to help you."

"Well...yeah," he said. "I'd be taking up your time and you don't even get paid for it. It's not a fair deal for you."

"As smart as you are, Jackson, you still have a lot to learn in life. If you work hard with me, in a relatively short period of time, you will wake up one day without an accent. When that happens, I will receive even more pleasure than you."

"I don't think that's possible, Mrs. Gray, but thank you. When can we start?"

"Don't thank me yet, Jackson. There are conditions with our arrangement. Your mother has to agree. You will also volunteer two hours a week at the library shelving returned books. And someday when an opportunity arises, promise me you will perform a like good deed for someone else.

"You have my promise, Mrs. Gray. And I keep my promises."

CHAPTER SEVEN

More often than not the last ten minutes of a high school biology class would border on perpetuity for Jackson. But sixty minutes wasn't nearly enough time for him to study a feminine subject named Claudia Foster in between taking notes. This was his second year at Silver Rock High and living in the same city, consecutive year records for him.

Jackson copied the teacher's blackboard notes in his notebook, then spied on Claudia. She filled out a tight sweater and straight skirt better than any sophomore girl in school. With striking blue eyes, perfect teeth, button nose, and a blonde hairdo, Claudia was pretty enough to be immortalized on a teen magazine cover. Nature, however, often had a way of evening things out. Claudia's IQ wasn't anywhere near as blessed as her measurements, which opened the door for her to take an interest in Jackson. She persuaded him with a big smile and a slight hip bump to help with her biology homework after school. The smile alone would have prompted a yes answer from him.

A rubber band whizzed past Jackson's ear. He twisted around in his desk chair to catch his pal, Junior, ready to launch another rubber band missile. Jackson ignored Junior to observe Claudia.

A rubber band nailed the back of Jackson's head. He gave his annoying friend an evil eye. Junior pantomimed dribbling a basketball with his right hand; a request to play in a pickup game after school at a church gym. Jackson answered with a headshake. Another rubber band spanked his head.

Claudia was busy filing her nails. Jackson chuckled to himself. He had become a proficient note taker thanks to Claudia. If he wasn't spending part of an afternoon with her, he was working at the market to help support his family, reading or volunteering his time at the public library, playing baseball at the park, basketball at the church, or helping his mother and brother at home. Aside from

Claudia, high school had become a bummer after he was cut from the baseball team - too many catchers who were better than he was. He studied enough to stay out of trouble with B's and C's.

Seconds after the bell rang, Claudia winked at Jackson and headed for the exit - a signal she wanted him to come to her house after school, even though they would be unsupervised. Her parent's owned a sporting goods store and didn't return to the house until dinner time. They lived on the right side of the tracks in a ritzy neighborhood. Their living room was almost as large as the house Jackson's mother had rented.

Jackson winked back. Their tutor-student relationship was on the QT; meaning they didn't socialize at school. Claudia was too busy flirting with seniors and being a member of the in-crowd to acknowledge him. He was fine with their arrangement. In high school sports, the leagues were based on ability, size, and age. With Claudia Foster, Jackson was out of his league. This had been his first opportunity to spend a few hours alone with a gorgeous teenage girl who was a lot worldlier than he was. He was under no illusion regarding his future with Claudia. If she passed biology with a C grade, it was only a matter of time before Claudia dropped him like a sizzling sausage hot off the grill. In the meantime, he would enjoy the experience while it lasted.

Jackson hurried to his locker after class. He spun the numbers to his combination lock, opened the metal door, and dumped his biology book onto the top shelf. Junior jabbed Jackson's side with a sharp elbow. Jackson retaliated with an elbow of his own.

"Hey man," Junior said, rubbing his shoulder. "You haven't played basketball with us for awhile. You're going to lose your touch."

"Don't have a choice. I've got to put my hours in at the market."

"I realize you have to work at the market to help out," Junior said. "What I'm talking about, when you aren't stocking and sweeping at the grocery store, instead of playing basketball and baseball with friends, you're trying to slip the salami into snooty Claudia."

Jackson grabbed a handful of Junior's shirt and slammed him into a locker. Junior knew better than to fight back.

"Keep your voice down, Junior. I told you in secret I was helping

Claudia with her homework. There's nothing going on. But if some-one hears you, the rumor will spread through school like a wildfire on a windy day."

"Come on, man. I'm concerned about you falling for her. No offense, Jackson, but Claudia can have any guy she wants. The tittle-tattle around school is she goes for guys who wear block sweaters and drive classy cars. You being with Claudia Foster is similar to drinking vanilla extract for the alcohol content - one way or another it's going to end up as a bad experience." Junior dropped a book into the locker. "Cute chicks like Jan and Elaine keep asking me about you. I'd like to date either one of them, 'cept they wouldn't go out with me. What I'm saying, you are playing with fire. Why go for the forbidden apple when you'd be better off picking a nice girl who is really interested in you?"

Jackson glanced down at his scruffy Keds. He couldn't afford to ask a girl out on a date. Or buy cool clothes. He wasn't old enough to get a driver's license yet, not that any gal would be seen with him in his mother's rattletrap station wagon. Claudia never mentioned anything about his clothes, but it was probably another reason why she didn't want to be seen with him at school. Someday he would have enough money to buy a whole closet full of cool clothes.

Jackson closed the locker door. Junior was right; he was playing with fire. Claudia's sexual come-ons were tempting, but he couldn't take the chance of getting into trouble. His mom had enough prob-lems keeping the landlord off their backs. Today would be his last tutoring session. Who would ever believe it was his decision to stop spending time with the foxiest girl in school?

"I'm sorry, Junior." Jackson shook his friend's hand. "Thanks for looking out for me. Instead of shooting baskets after school, why don't we go to the church now? We can have the whole court to ourselves."

"Wish I could, man, but I can't cut classes the way you do, Jackson." Junior rubbed a pimple on his forehead. "I don't have a sweet deal like the one you worked out with your boss and school counselor to cut classes."

The last warning bell rang. They split in different directions. If Jackson hustled, he would be seated at his English class desk on time. Or he could spend an hour at the library talking to Mrs. Gray, without an accent.

Jackson made a quick right turn and headed for the exit.

CHAPTER EIGHT

Jackson shelved the last can of dog food from the case with a sense of sadness. Alpo had been Mickey's favorite. So much had changed in his life in the last two weeks. Claudia Foster was no longer in the picture. His brother Jim's heart trouble had taken a turn for the worse, and his mother had given their dog away because they couldn't afford to keep a pet. Someday Jackson would earn enough money to fix Jim's heart, wine and dine a girlfriend, and feed a pet dog filet mignon.

Jackson stepped back to examine the aisle for any label crooked or out of place. One of his high school buddies razzed him about working for a Jew. Jackson was so grateful to have the job and a boss as nice and fair as Mr. Ornstein, he'd don a yarmulke if asked.

He closed his eyes to combat the sting from working late hours. Stocking product and cleaning at night for the Reno store's morning opening was a never ending chore. He knew his job so well he could do it in his sleep - and probably had.

Satisfied with his work, Jackson began to break down empty boxes. *"Sugar Shack,"* a current 1963 hit song by Jimmy Gilmore and the Fireballs, played on his transistor radio. He didn't bother to look up when he heard a familiar *click, click* sound from the store owner's tapped shoes.

"Jackson, may I please have a word with you?" Mr. Ornstein said with a slight European accent, waving a handful of invoices.

"Sure, Mr. O, what can I do for you?" Jackson dropped the cardboard onto the shiny linoleum floor and straightened up. He switched off the transistor radio.

Mr. Ornstein admired Jackson's work with a smile and a nod. He was always polite to his employees and the customers, yet shrewd and tough as a businessman - most of the time. Even an intelligent person like Mr. Ornstein had a few blind spots.

"How the heck did you get our Ajax Meat Company rep to

discount their prices?" Mr. Ornstein pointed his index finger at the top invoice. "I could never get them to budge."

"When the Ajax rep walked into the store last week I happened to be holding a Reeder's Meats box. I faked an attempt to hide the box behind my back, but he caught me. I thought he'd have a cow when he assumed we were ordering from his competitor."

"I don't understand, Jackson. You know our only meat vender is Ajax Meat Company. They have a greater selection and the quality of their product is far better than Reeder's."

"You know that, Mr. O, and I know that, but clearly the Ajax rep didn't want to lose part or all of our business. A slight goose was all he needed."

"Where did you get the Reeder's Meats box?" Mr. Ornstein exposed a palm.

"I picked up the Reeder's box from the back alley of the grocery store across town." Jackson grinned. "Your handshake agreement from way back with Ajax gave them a product exclusive. Unfortunately, they have been taking advantage of your loyalty. Loyalty goes both ways. I didn't lie to him, Mr. O. I never said we were buying from Reeder's."

With a hand on his stomach, Mr. Ornstein's body shook with laughter. He folded the invoices, stuffed them into his back pocket, and wiped elated tears away with a finger.

"My boy, you have been blessed with a natural gift for doing business. Keep this up and you will have your own chain of supermarkets by the time you graduate from high school - if you graduate from high school. This afternoon, I received a distressing phone call from your school counselor."

"Uh-oh. I can explain, Mr. O."

"We understand you have to work extra hours to help your mother out, especially now with Jim's illness - a damn shame for someone so young to have a bum heart. You even work on your birthday. I gave you the day off to see the new Hitchcock movie, 'The Birds and the Bees.'"

"It's just 'The Birds,' Mr. O. Really, I don't mind working on my birthday. And thank you again for my gifts."

Jackson patted his front pocket holding a ten dollar bill, plus two boxes of unwrapped baseball cards. Best sixteenth birthday presents he could ever get.

"My pleasure, Jackson. Let me remind you, your counselor and I made a deal you would keep up your attendance and studies while working for me. She said you have been missing many of your classes. Yet, in spite of that, you are passing all of your tests and getting C's and B's. She found this to be rather amazing. Without actually saying you cheated on those tests, her words alluded to that effect."

"I'm sorry, Mr. O. I didn't mean to let you down. What did you say to my counselor?"

"I told her you are the most honest, loyal, and brightest employee I have ever had, and intelligent enough to pass those tests on your own. Which one of us is correct, Jackson?"

Jackson exhaled a deep breath. He was grateful Mr. Ornstein defended him. He had failed this wonderful man who had been nothing but nice to him since the day he walked into the store and asked for a job.

"I hate to say this," Jackson said, staring down at the floor, "but both of you are wrong."

"I do not understand." Mr. Ornstein's accent suddenly became thicker as he placed his hand on Jackson's shoulder. "Please explain what you are saying?"

"I didn't cheat. And I'm nowhere near as worthy as what you described to my school counselor." Jackson met Mr. Ornstein's eyes. A recent growth spurt made him stand a smidgeon taller than the owner. "I found out from other students what the tests covered and crammed the night before. There are more interesting places to learn stuff, including this grocery store, than sitting bored in a classroom."

"Ah, yes. Going to the library to immerse yourself in newspapers and fictional books. Or to play sports. And, of course, flirting with pretty vixen Claudia Foster." Mr. Ornstein cleared his throat. "Playing hooky for nookie will get you nowhere, Jackson. Especially with Claudia. As attractive as that girl is, she's not right in the head. I hate to sound like a parent, but with your God-given good looks, you can have any gal you want."

Jackson felt his cheeks heat up. He had stopped seeing Claudia, but not before her father came home early two weeks ago and caught them in bed. Claudia propositioned him after he informed her he was ending their tutoring sessions. He first refused, afraid of getting into trouble. Claudia coerced him into a corner where having sex with her would be the lesser of his evils.

Jackson held back a smile. He wasn't one bit sorry Claudia forced him into going all the way. His first sexual experience proved to be so pleasurable and satisfying it quashed any doubt he had about his sexuality after being raped by Dalton Peppers. Surprisingly, Jackson had soon been ready for another romp when Claudia's father walked into the bedroom, before rushing out to get his shotgun. Jackson grabbed his clothes and escaped through the bedroom window.

Mr. Ornstein shook Jackson's arm, bringing him back to their discussion.

"You will never be sorry about getting an education." Mr. Ornstein tapped a finger to his temple. "Work hard, get your schooling in, and find a nice girl to settle down with."

"I'm always appreciative when you offer advice, Mr. O. You have provided me an education I could never get in school. You've shared many of your secrets of success and educated me on how to operate a business. You also taught me what the word autonomy means. I can do it my way as long as I don't stray from the boundaries you set. What I appreciate the most though, is you have always treated me and my family with respect."

"Thank you for those kind words, Jackson. It seems like we learn from each other, but you need the basic school principles to—"

A series of heavy knocks came from the front door. Mr. Ornstein raised his hands in the air, and removed a pocket watch from his vest. He twisted the watch's knob several times to make sure the time piece was running.

"Someday, grocery markets will be open twenty-four hours," Mr. Ornstein said. "But that day isn't here yet. You see, Jackson, this is another example of why you should attend all of your classes. It's obvious the person knocking at our door is desperate, has a complaint, or can't read our *CLOSED* sign on the door." He headed for the entrance. "I'll get it. You finish up with what you were doing and go home, eat some birthday cake, and get your rest."

Bells pealed when Mr. Ornstein unlocked and opened the front door. It had to be someone in dire need of something. Jackson kneeled to collect the cardboard and rose to his feet when he heard his name being called out. A uniformed policeman marched towards him with Mr. Ornstein's tapped shoes struggling to keep up.

"Are you Jackson Kingman?" the officer asked.

Jackson's stomach rumbled. Damn. The cop must be here because of Jackson's truancy. Why would the police come after him at nine o'clock at night for non-attendance? Maybe Mr. Ornstein set Jackson up to teach him a lesson.

"I'm Jackson Kingman, officer. I admit to missing several of my classes. As you can see, I work a lot of hours to help support my mother and brother. I promise perfect attendance from here on out. Mr. Ornstein already enlightened me on the subject."

"Jackson, I have a warrant for your arrest." The policeman removed a paper from his inside coat pocket. "I'm sorry it has to be at this hour. Better this way than pulling you out of a classroom in front of the other students."

"For cutting classes?"

"Jackson, the warrant is for having sexual relations with an underage girl. In this state, sex with a minor is considered to be statutory rape whether it's consensual or not."

"I didn't rape anyone."

"It is my understanding," the officer said, "Mr. Lucius Foster caught you in his house having sex with his daughter who is a sophomore in high school."

"Officer Stahl," Mr. Ornstein said, "I remember a time when I caught a fifteen year old boy stealing prophylactics from my store. Do you recall the incident, Stevey?"

"How could I forget, Mr. Ornstein? You made me sweep the store floors, wash windows, and dump garbage for a week in lieu of not telling my parents. I learned my lesson - never stole anything again. Maybe that's why I became a cop."

"Just like you, Stevey, Jackson is a good boy who made a mistake," Mr. Ornstein said.

"I'm doing my job, Mr. Ornstein." Officer Stahl produced a gritty expression as he pulled a pair of handcuffs from his belt and encircled them around Jackson's wrists. "I'm sorry, Jackson. I've never met a teenage boy, including myself, who wasn't horny. I sure hope you don't get Judge Dragon at your preliminary hearing."

Jackson swallowed hard. Mr. Ornstein closed his eyes and shook his head. Rather than fulfilling his boss's prophecy of being a successful businessman, he might spend his adulthood in prison with a number on his back, bartering cigarettes with inmates. The metal handcuffs were painful on his wrists and dignity. What hurt more was the thought he had let down his poor mother and Mr. O. His mother had enough to fret about with a low paying job and Jim's doctor bills. If he was sentenced to jail, it could ruin his family.

"Officer Stahl, I'm sure there is a way we can make a deal similar to what Mr. Ornstein offered when you were my age," Jackson said.

"Sorry, Jackson." The officer shook his head. "I would if I could."

"I'm totally screwed." Jackson was escorted to the front door.

"That is exactly what got you in this mess in the first place, Jackson." Mr. Ornstein said. "Don't worry. I will help you if I can."

Jackson shook his head. If he allowed Mr. O. to help, it might impugn the stellar reputation his employer earned in the community. There had to be a way for Jackson to get out of this mess on his own.

CHAPTER NINE

The Kingman kitchen table was filled with serious hardbound tomes, journals, and periodicals. Jackson's mother pushed a book aside and placed a grilled cheese sandwich and full glass of milk in front of him. He ignored the food and kept writing on a pad of lined school paper.

Jim sat across the table from Jackson with his head buried in one of the books Jackson had asked him to review. Inept on the ball field, Jim starred as a student. His poor brother looked frail, but he was a willing player on team Jackson - as long as his endurance held up - to help create a strategy for the upcoming hearing two days away. A strategy that necessitated understanding state, county, and city laws and regulations.

Jackson's mom thrust an open hand with pills in front of Jim before handing him a glass of apple juice. She stayed by Jim's side until he swallowed his medication.

"We haven't talked about what you did," she said to Jackson. "You're too young to be involved in a S E X U A L orgy."

"I can spell, Mother," Jim said, without looking up from his book.

"The last thing I wanted to do was let you down, Mom. I'm sorry."

"Not just me, Jackson. Mr. Ornstein is a well respected person in this community. He got you out of jail on your own recognizance. Is this how you pay him back? By stealing? Several of these books are not supposed to be removed from the library. They're going to put you in jail and squirt glue in the keyhole so you will never get out."

"Mom, Mrs. Gray the librarian gave me permission to take these books home for Jim and me to study after I promised to bring them back. Mrs. Gray was the one who picked them out for me and marked what I should read. She knows when I make a promise, I keep it. She'll be at the hearing along with Mr. Ornstein."

"Oh, no. Now you have implicated your brother, the nice lady from the library, and Mr. Ornstein." She sat down at the table. "I hope the jail is big enough for another person. At least family and good friends will all be together. What do you want me to do?"

Jackson exchanged a smile with Jim. He opened a journal to a marked page and slid it to his mother along with a pad of paper.

"Please read this section and tell me if it's pertinent to what I'm being charged with. If you're not sure, write it down anyway. We will discuss it later."

His mother started reading silently with her lips moving. The whole Kingman family was on the case. Jackson's eyes focused on the page he had been reading.

"Jackson," Jim said in an excited voice. "I think I found something…"

CHAPTER TEN

Jackson sat alone at a table fronting an empty elevated judge's bench and picked at his sore cuticles. For a second time, he would face a judge who had the power to change the course of his life in a negative way. The Reno courtroom was larger and more sobering than Judge Lane's chambers from four years ago in West Virginia when he was a twelve year old boy. Now he was two years away from being draft board eligible for an all expense paid trip to the jungles of Vietnam. Or a few minutes away from a prison's free room and board. Some choice.

The bailiff worked a newspaper's crossword puzzle at a floor level station next to where the judge would sit. Jackson peered over his shoulder to ensure his mother, brother, Mr. Ornstein, and Mrs. Gray were still sitting behind him in the gallery. Mr. Foster and his daughter Claudia camped out on the opposite side.

Jackson rubbed the tender skin areas where handcuffs had imprisoned his wrists. He had been released from jail on his own recognizance after Mr. Ornstein intervened. Mr. O offered to pay for a lawyer to represent Jackson if the case proceeded to trial. Jackson refused the generous offer. He was dead set on fending for himself.

Jackson glanced down at his best clothes; chinos, a white shirt covered by a blue V-neck sweater vest, and brown loafers. Mr. Ornstein and Claudia's father were decked out in suits and ties. Claudia wore a plain white dress, with her blonde hair pulled back into pigtails. Did the church dress his mother had on have one more good luck prayer?

Jackson could use all the luck he could find, starting with not getting Judge Dragon as the residing judge. He flinched when the door embedded into the back wall opened. A black robed man with a somber face entered the courtroom without looking at Jackson. Why do judges wear black robes? Maybe in the old days they hid weapons for protection. The judge placed a wood nameplate at the front of his bench. Jackson's chin fell into his chest.

"All rise," the bailiff announced, "for the Honorable Darnell Dragon." He waited until the Judge took his chair. "Please be seated."

"Damn," Jackson muttered. His legs trembled. He just received strike one before the game even started.

Judge Dragon studied several pages of paper. The part in the judge's short dark hair was crooked and his bushy eyebrows scrunched together to almost meet in the center. He finally placed the papers down on the bench and stared at Jackson.

"Jackson Kingman, do you know what an arraignment is?"

"Yes, your honor. It's a trial before the trial so a judge can decide how to proceed."

"Correct, Mr. Kingman," The judge said, with a nod. "Have you had previous experience in a courtroom before a judge?"

"No, your honor," Jackson said in a shaky voice. Not a lie since his family convened in Judge Lane's chambers. "I went to the library and studied up."

"Very impressive, Mr. Kingman. Have you retained an attorney to represent you if this case goes to court?"

"No sir."

"Do you want a court appointed attorney from the DA's office?"

"No sir."

Jackson's mother cried out. Judge Dragon's eyes scolded her outburst, and he returned his gaze to Jackson.

"Mr. Kingman, as a sixteen year old in this state, you are considered to be an adult. You have been charged with having sexual intercourse with an underage female; a crime that is considered to be misdemeanor statutory rape. Do you understand the seriousness of the offense you are accused of?"

"Yes, your honor."

"What was the purpose of your unsupervised visit to Miss Foster's house?"

"For several weeks I had been helping Miss Foster with her biology homework."

"A wiseacre response, Mr. Kingman? Or was that a reference to school assignments?"

"School assignments. Miss Foster was having trouble with biology and other classes."

"Very well," the judge said. "Let's get on with this. How do you plead, Mr. Kingman?"

"May I ask a question, your honor?" Jackson put his hands into his pants pockets to hide the tremble. He had not peed-his-pants since he was four years old, but the urge was almost overwhelming.

"Since you have done your homework at the library, you should be aware this is not a hearing for defending your case."

"Yes, your honor, I'm aware of that. May I still ask a question?"

"Is this a kangaroo court, Judge?" Mr. Foster shouted. "How long do we have to listen to this punk who stole the bloom from a naïve high school sophomore girl against her will?"

"Although I understand the emotion behind your comments, Mr. Foster, please do not interrupt the proceedings again, otherwise I will hold you in contempt." The judge jiggled a finger at Jackson. "You may ask your question, Mr. Kingman."

"What is the court's definition of rape, your honor?"

"Not the question I thought you would ask." The judge straightened his papers. "Rape can be defined as forcing someone to have sex against their will. However, in your case, anyone sixteen years old or older that has sexual intercourse with a minor - minor being defined in this state as a person under the age of sixteen - is considered statutory rape. Two different charges, but make no mistake, Mr. Kingman, both are despicable acts."

"Based on your definitions, judge, rape and statutory rape were committed," Jackson said. "I plead not guilty."

"With all due respect, Mr. Kingman, you admitted to committing rape and statutory rape. Why would you plead not guilty when a no contest plea would be in order?"

"Your honor, I'll plead no contest to a moral wrong of having sex before marriage," Jackson said. "I never said I raped Claudia... ah, Miss Foster by any definition. But make no mistake, sir, rape and statutory rape were committed. I was the one who had sex against my will. Furthermore—"

Judge Dragon emitted a sharp laugh, ran a hand through his hair, messing the part even more. From behind, Jackson could hear his troubled mother conversing with Mr. Ornstein. His boss attempted to calm her down, but his tone lacked conviction.

"Can you believe this guy?" Mr. Foster's voice carried from the gallery. "Jackson Kingman should never be allowed to see the light of day again for the rest of his life."

"That is enough, Mr. Foster," the judge announced, pointing the gavel at Jackson. "In all my years on the bench, I have never heard such absurdity. Out of sheer curiosity, Mr. Kingman, how is it possible for a female to rape a male against his will?"

"You should ask Miss Foster that question, your honor," Jackson said, turning towards Claudia. "Next you should ask her—"

"Do not tell me what I should or should not do in my courtroom, Mr. Kingman." The judge pounded his gavel three times, rose to his feet, and leaned forward with glaring eyes. "You will not make a mockery out of this arraignment. I have listened to your drivel long enough." Judge Dragon switched his sights to Claudia and offered a sympathetic smile. "Miss Foster, the court apologizes for what just transpired. Bailiff, take Jackson Kingman to a jail cell where he belongs."

The bailiff jumped to his feet with the chair sliding backwards. His hand reached for handcuffs on the way to Jackson. Jackson's first inclination was to flee the courtroom as fast as he could. Instead, he marched up to the bench. Judge Dragon's eyes widened.

"Judge," Jackson said, "Claudia Foster is not a minor. Furthermore, I turned sixteen five days ago, which means I was fifteen when our sex took place. Claudia has been sixteen years old for over five months. She's a sophomore in high school because she had to repeat a school grade. Furthermore, Claudia said she would tell the world I raped her if I didn't have sex with her. I know it was wrong, Judge. But I was scared. Scared she would spread rumors to hurt me and my family."

The bailiff roughly twisted Jackson's arms behind his back. Jackson could feel the hurt of the suffocating cuffs before they made contact with his wrists. Judge Dragon's grimace told him everything he needed to know. Not even Perry Mason could get him out of the mess he created for himself. His pal Junior's words came to mind. He played with fire and got scorched.

"Wait a minute, bailiff," the judge ordered. "Miss Foster, I see you have your purse with you. Are you a licensed driver?"

"Ah...yeah, sure Judge. What does my driver's license have to do with anything?"

"We're leaving, Claudia." Mr. Foster pulled on her arm. "You're not on trial here."

"Stop right there," the judge barked. "Miss Foster, please bring your license to me. I want to verify your age."

"I won't allow you to impugn my daughter's reputation by—"

"Oh shut up, Daddy," Claudia screamed. "This is what you get by making me come here today and miss cheerleader tryouts. For your information, I lost my *bloom* when I was fourteen. Jackson told you the truth, Judge. I'm sixteen years old. Every boy in school would do anything to screw me, but not Jackson. Believe me, he wanted to, but he was afraid we would get caught and it would harm his family. First time anyone ever turned me down, which really pissed me off to no end. So I threatened him by saying I would tell everyone he raped me if he wouldn't do the deed."

Judge Dragon plopped down in his chair and slammed the gavel as if he was hammering a nail. The fingers on his free hand massaged the lines in his forehead.

"This hearing will not proceed any further. I want to see you Mr. Foster and your daughter Claudia in my chambers immediately." The judge's features softened. "With sincere apologies, Mr. Kingman, I can see why you didn't want to be represented. No attorney could have provided a better defense than you did. Where I do not personally approve of pre-martial sex, Miss Foster's admission explained your reluctance and how she coerced you into the act. You are dismissed of all charges, Mr. Kingman." He raised the gavel in the air, then pointed the head at Jackson. "However, you are within your rights to charge Miss Foster for rape."

"Thank you, Judge. Your willingness to get to the truth is all the right I deserve."

The judge left the back wall door open for the Fosters to enter his chambers. Jackson turned to greet his fan club in the gallery. He never wanted to see another courtroom again for the rest of his life. Claudia's father blocked his path.

"You took advantage of my daughter and now you've screwed with me," Mr. Foster spit out. "Ever see what a shotgun blast does to a human body, Kingman? If you remain in this town, your days and your family's days are numbered. Not an idle threat, boy. It's a very sincere promise I aim to keep."

Jackson flashed on his father lying near death, riddled with buckshot holes; his lowlife uncles in Judge Lane's chambers; and the face of a sexual pervert named Dalton Peppers. Would there ever be a time in his life when the agenda driven behavior, threats, and warnings would stop? Probably not, but those individuals who choose to denigrate or challenge him unfairly will quickly learn their actions will receive a radically different response. Starting now.

Jackson's fist struck pay dirt by burrowing deep into Foster's soft belly, sending Claudia's father to the floor gagging for air. Jackson turned and smiled at his supporters. The Fosters had learned a valuable lesson today. Threats, physical or voiced, would only motivate Jackson to work harder to win.

CHAPTER ELEVEN

The Treasure Island Naval Base Officer's Club buzzed with activity for a Wednesday night. Jackson delivered the dinner check to a pair of captains and walked away with a healthy tip. During the day he wore a white hat as a twenty-one year old 2nd class petty officer in the navy. Three nights a week he also worked as a waiter at the Officer's Club. His brother Jim's heart problem was getting worse. Jackson sent most of his waiter earnings and navy pay to his mother to help cover mounting doctor bills.

"King!"

Jackson turned to the bar. It still felt weird being called King rather than Kingman. The bartender, a moonlighting chief petty officer who was trying to support four kids on a military salary, motioned Jackson over with a hand wave. He had a serious, tight lipped expression on his face instead of his usual jovial demeanor. Without saying a word he pushed a tray with two drinks to Jackson and pointed to a table in the corner. A familiar aroma from one of the drinks made Jackson's mouth water for a sip. Wild Turkey was his favorite. He would have to wait until his shift was over when the chief would sneak him a freebie or two.

Jackson balanced the tray with one hand and headed to the table. Before joining the navy, he legally changed his name, but avoided having his picture posted in a newspaper, much to the chagrin of his navy recruiter. Jackson even talked his mother and brother into changing their last name to King, then moved them to another town in Nevada. If Claudia Foster's father followed through on his shotgun threat, it would be a difficult task to track down any of the former Kingmans. The same was true for his uncles or anyone else from West Virginia. Jackson vowed to keep their name change a secret for life.

Jackson nodded in recognition when he noticed who had ordered the drinks. His commanding officer, Lieutenant Commander

Thomas Oliver, was sitting alone in civvies. The commander must be waiting for his wife or a fellow officer. Jackson had developed several friendships with the brass, another benefit from working at the Officer's Club. The old saying, it's not what you know but who you know played true on the base, especially if the who you knew had a whole lot of braids on their hat.

"Good evening, King," the commander said in an officer-like tone.

"Commander Oliver." Jackson placed the drinks at opposite ends of the table. "A gin and tonic for you, sir. And, if my nose isn't betraying me, a Wild Turkey for your guest who has great taste in whiskey."

"Let's dispense with military protocol crap, Jackson. Have a seat. I need to talk to you."

Jackson hesitated. Commander Oliver's serious tone took him by surprise. First the chief, now his off duty buddy. Ollie was usually upbeat and never snooty like some of the officers. Maybe he had a fight with his wife, which wouldn't be unusual. Jackson was often a sounding board for Ollie's vents.

"You know I can't sit with you, Ollie," Jackson said in a low voice. "I'm working my shift and enlisted men aren't allowed to eat or drink in the officer's club. But I appreciate the offer."

"Sit down, Jackson. That is an order." The commander took a long gulp from his gin and tonic. "As of right now, you're taking a break as a waiter and officially a guest of mine. If you're worried about your job here, I cleared it with your restaurant supervisor. Look, it's not like we don't hang out together drinking or playing ball. You've been to my house for dinner more times than I can count and never once complained about my wife's shitty cooking. That alone makes you as good a friend as I've ever had in the navy."

A joke, but there was no smile in Ollie's eyes. Jackson sat down, ogled the shot of Wild Turkey, and looked for a tell from Ollie. Something strange was going on. This was the first time Ollie blatantly crossed the status line between officers and enlisted men, knowing full well Jackson could get into some serious trouble sitting at a table in the officer's club - double that if he was drinking. Whatever Ollie wanted to talk to him about had to be important.

It couldn't be to send Jackson on some kind of secret mission; a navy yeoman handled administration and clerical work. Hopefully, the subject of his friend's behavior wasn't concerning a divorce or separation. He was equally fond of Olivia even if she couldn't cook. Jackson swallowed hard. Or maybe this was about something he had been deflecting for a while.

"I value our friendship as much as you do, Ollie," Jackson said. "However, if this is about giving me my shipping over lecture, forget it. In eight months my four year commitment will be up. I've had duty in Kodiak, Alaska and Lemoore Naval Air Station. Sorry, this is my last stop and I have no desire to re-up to stay in the navy. After I get my honorable discharge, I'm going to take a government free ride to school with the GI bill or I will seek my fortune in the business world, but I am not re-upping."

Jackson's right hand squeezed into a fist so he couldn't grasp the shot glass. His weakness for alcohol was becoming more and more prevalent each day; shades of his father. Some of his morning hangovers were horrendous, but he always managed to get through the day. He could stop drinking if he wanted to, but he had no desire to quit. His left hand gripped the table. Was Ollie here because his drinking was out of control?

"My mission tonight isn't to get you to ship over for another tour of duty." Ollie swiped another gulp. "Truth be known, I'd be doing you a disservice if I did. Look, Jackson, you are smart as a whip and the most four-0, squared away enlisted man I've ever run across. I'm not talking about your work as a yeoman. Aside from being a natural leader, you have the ability to get things done efficiently and quickly. It's no secret I give you assignments that would normally go to my junior officers. I'm not pushing, but if you have any inkling about staying in the navy, I'd highly recommend you go to Officer's Candidate School. Say the word, Jackson, and I can get you in."

"Thanks for your support, Ollie, but my plans for the future have nothing to do with the navy. Now I've got to get back to work before the wrong person sees me."

Jackson got to his feet and scoped out a sea of occupied dining tables. The room's ambiance was alive with chatter, but none of the diners stared back at him - a good sign. If he wasn't already on report, maybe he got lucky.

"Sit down, Jackson." Ollie pushed the Wild Turkey inches closer to him. "I'm here as your commanding officer and friend. I've got some bad news for you. There's no easy way of saying this. Your brother Jim passed away."

Jackson fell into his seat. All action surrounding him slowed in motion. How could Jim be dead? His mother's last letter said the doctor was encouraged about how Jim was reacting to his new medication. The shot of Wild Turkey became distorted from tears clouding Jackson's eyes. He flashed on Jim as a boy reading a book or dropping a fly ball. Maybe Ollie was mistaken. Maybe it was someone else's brother Jim.

"Sorry, buddy. I know this comes as a shock. A military hookup flight is being arranged if not tonight, tomorrow at the latest." Ollie reached into his wallet and handed Jackson a folded hundred dollar bill. "Emergency money. Take it. It doesn't matter if it's my emergency or yours, that's what it's there for. You need to be with your mother."

Jackson lifted the shot glass to his lips and tilted it until the amber colored whiskey was gone in one swallow. A familiar warm sensation filled his throat and chest. His heartbeat was out of control, but the drink brought most of his senses back into play. Ollie was right. Since he joined the navy, his mother's sole mission had been to take care of Jim. She must be beside herself. He had to get to Nevada as soon as possible.

"Thank you, Ollie." Benjamin Franklin stared back at Jackson. "This will help with the funeral. I'll pay you back when I can. I can't believe Jim is gone."

"Let's call it even." Ollie folded Jackson's fingers over the bill. "It wipes my slate clean from all the backgammon, darts, gin rummy, and one-on-one basketball games I lost to you. Take care of your mother. I'll tend to the red tape and brass."

Jackson's stomach barked. His head was about to explode. He was experiencing conflicted emotions; grief for the most gentle person he had ever known and overwhelming anger for life's unfairness. Maybe Jim would still be alive if Jackson had stayed in Nevada.

"King! What the hell do you think you're doing in here, drinking no less?"

Lieutenant Jerome Figg was in uniform, hands on his hips, glaring at Jackson. Figg was the last person on the island base Jackson wanted to see. The lieutenant thought the bars on his collar were like deodorant for a stinky personality, especially when he was dealing with individuals he outranked.

"Stand down, Figg," the commander said. "I asked Jackson to meet me here, I'll explain later. This is none of your business."

"With all due respect, sir," Figg said, "2nd Class Petty Officer King should be written up for being in an officers club imbibing hard liquor. It's bad enough we have to put up with his insubordination and lack of proper respect towards his superior officers." He pointed a finger at Jackson. "I'm putting you on report, sailor. Your E-5 rank is now history. I hope they demote you to seaman recruit as well as giving you a long stay in the brig."

"You're out of line, Figg." The commander rose to his feet. "I'll take care of this, Jackson. Get out of here and prepare for the immediacy of the assignment we discussed."

Jackson glared up at Figg. The lieutenant was still pissed off about the officers versus enlisted men softball game after Jackson ran over Figg when the dumbshit tried to block him from scoring at home plate. Figg conveniently forgot there was no collar or bars on his softball jersey.

"Commander Oliver, I realize this slug is your pet petty officer—"

Jackson fired out of his chair as if he was driven by a spring. He sent a hard right-cross to Figg's chin, sending him to the hardwood floor. Jackson didn't hesitate to jump on the stunned lieutenant and pummel his face with punches. Ollie and another person pulled Jackson off of Figg before the navy was minus one skinny lieutenant.

"Call the MP's!" Figg rose to his feet while wiping blood from his mouth and nose. "I want this son of a bitch arrested and sent to the brig."

Ollie grabbed Jackson's arm and tugged him towards the exit. All eyes in the bar and restaurant were focused on Jackson. Figg got what was coming to him, but his timing couldn't have been worse.

"Bad move, buddy," Ollie said. "That was exactly what Figg wanted you to do. I told you I would take care of it. Too many people saw you hit him. There's only so much I can do at this point. Pack your gear as quickly as you can. I'll get you off this island tonight if I have to fly you myself, but you'll have to face some kind of discipline when you get back - maybe even a demotion. The navy has a low tolerance for an enlisted man hitting an officer, even off duty. We can only hope in eight months your discharge is honorable, otherwise your chances for using GI Bill for school might go the same route as the Titanic."

CHAPTER TWELVE

Jackson's stomach growled loud enough for the receptionist to peer up at him from her desk. He squirmed in the lobby chair. The belly rumble wasn't from emptiness; only a case of pre-job interview jitters.

It wasn't difficult to figure out why he was nervous. After leaving the navy with a General Discharge, thanks to Lieutenant Figg, Jackson's San Francisco nondescript jobs included department store clerk, telephone solicitor, and waiter. Lloyd Outdoor's employment announcement in the *San Francisco Chronicle Classified Want Ads* jumped out at him like a freshly painted billboard; this was the career opportunity he had been seeking.

The receptionist opened her mouth to say something to Jackson when the desk phone rang. He straightened the crease in his slacks and adjusted the tie knotted tight into his white dress shirt collar. His eyes once again shifted to the wall clock located behind the receptionist desk. He arrived fifteen minutes early, which meant he'd been waiting for thirty minutes. Maybe this was a pre-interview test to assess his patience and how much he wanted this job? Or maybe the interviewee before him was wooing the position away from Jackson. His stomach growled again.

The lobby was lackluster at best with no plants, pictures, awards, or dressy office furniture, with the exception of the attractive receptionist who was old enough to be his mother. The phone receiver was pinned to her ear with one hand while she scribbled on a notepad with the other. She replaced the phone to its base after transferring the call.

"Sorry for the wait, Mr. King," she said. "Mr. Lloyd will be with you shortly."

"Thank you, Ma'am. My mother used to say all good things were worth waiting for. However, an adage she often forgot the meaning of when I came home late from play."

"Sounds like a case of mother's prerogative, not that I would know." Her smile turned downward. "Can I get you a cup of coffee? Some water? A sedative?"

"It's that obvious, huh." He laughed. "Thanks for the offer, ma'am, but no thank you. Please call me Jackson and tell me about what Mr. Lloyd is looking for in an applicant."

"Well, Jackson, you may call me Rose." Her green eyes sparkled. "I have been with Lloyd Outdoor for a long time. No other applicant has ever asked me that question. Andrew Lloyd is smart, kind, fair, and generous to a fault. You can't tell by our office decor, but he's a first class kind of guy away from the office. But our workplace is merely that - a no frills place to get the job done. He gives his people autonomy and the opportunity for advancement, unless they can't handle it."

"The Peter Principle," Jackson offered.

"I beg your pardon," Rose said, with a confused smile.

"In work situations, the Peter Principle is a concept where some employees rise to their level of incompetence. In other words, being a skilled carpenter doesn't necessarily equip a person to excel at a higher level as a foreman, manager, or contractor."

"Thank you for enlightening me, Jackson. How did you come about learning this?"

"By observing guys in the service and working various jobs," he said. "I recognized a like tendency in many people, but I could never put an actual name to it. A librarian referred me to a book written by Laurence Peter - who created a double entendre title and concept by adding the word principle behind his last name."

"I'm impressed. Mr. Lloyd is looking to groom a young person who wants to be here for the long haul. I think the military uses the term 'lifer.' A quick learner who is willing to work as many hours as it takes to gain practical knowledge of the outdoor business and to eventually run this company. Does the term Peter Principle apply to you, Jackson?"

Jackson leaned back into his chair, crossed his legs, and blew out a relieved breath. This charming woman was better than Alka-Seltzer.

"I'm the opposite of the Peter Principle employee, Rose. The ladders I want to climb will require extensions. All I'm asking for is a chance to prove myself."

Jackson wasn't as good as he advertised, but he would work a hundred times harder to make his bold statement become true. Hopefully, Rose understood he wasn't a cocky blowhard trying to impress her with false rhetoric.

The desk phone buzzed. Rose buzzed back twice and stood for the first time. She hand motioned to Jackson it was show time.

"I'll escort you to Mr. Lloyd's office. Good luck, Jackson. I mean that sincerely."

Jackson followed Rose to an open office door. In high heels she was an inch shorter than him. It was too bad his new friend wasn't doing the hiring.

"Knock, knock," she said, entering the office. "Jackson King is here for his interview."

Rose left the room, closing the door behind her. Andrew Lloyd shook Jackson's hand and took a chair opposite from him in front of the desk. He was wearing an expensive brown suit, vest, and shiny brown shoes probably worth more than Jackson's whole wardrobe. His thinning hair was graying at the sides and his waist had given way to middle-age spread. Jackson zeroed in on the man's light blue eyes.

"I see on your application, Jackson," Lloyd said, pointing a forefinger at the form, "you grew up in Nevada before enlisting in the navy. I can't imagine there are many naval recruiters in a state that has no bordering oceans. What made you choose a four year hitch wearing a white hat?"

Mr. Lloyd's first question threw him off a bit. Should Jackson open up and say he had to get his ass out of Nevada before Claudia Foster's father fulfilled a promise to use him as target practice? Or declare he changed his last name before joining the navy so as not to leave a trail for Mr. Foster or anyone from West Virginia to find him? Based on Rose's description, Mr. Lloyd appeared to be an understanding man, but revealing his background would probably send Jackson to the front door jobless. For the sake of this interview, he would share the other reason he enlisted in the navy.

"Sir, I joined that branch of the service so I wouldn't get drafted into the army. I have a dislike for guns."

"So I take it you are not much of a hunter for sport."

"No sir. How sporting is it if an animal doesn't have the means to shoot back?"

"Couldn't agree with you more," Lloyd said. "Did you see much of the world on Uncle Sam's dime?"

"Well, sir, if you call Kodiak, Alaska, Lemoore Naval Air Station near Fresno, and Treasure Island Naval Base here in San Francisco seeing the world, I'll say yes."

"I have always admired the men and women who have served in our armed forces," Lloyd said. "What kind of duty did you have in Kodiak, Alaska?"

"Mostly we monitored Russian plane and ship activity."

"Sounds like tough duty," Lloyd said with a grin.

"Mr. Lloyd, I don't want you to think I'm taking all the credit or I have a big head, but I'm proud to say not one Russian plane or boat attacked us while I was there."

Andrew Lloyd gave Jackson a quizzical look, slapped his knee with the application, and burst out laughing.

"Thank you, Jackson. I needed that. You demonstrated one of your strengths. Tell me what your weakness is?"

Jackson ran a hand over his mouth. He could answer women, alcohol, tobacco, and a temper he was learning to control. Or he could turn a negative into a positive.

"I don't mind sharing this with you, Mr. Lloyd. No matter what success I've had, I'm never content. I'm driven to get better."

"I see you've worked several jobs after leaving the navy. What drove you to leave them?"

"Different reasons," Jackson said. "I was the top money raiser as a phone solicitor for the blind. After doing some research, I discovered the products I was selling weren't actually made by local blind people, but produced cheaply in a foreign country. When I confronted the owner, he fired me." Jackson grinned. "The Better Business Bureau found what I discovered interesting enough to close them down."

"What about the waiter job?" Lloyd asked.

"Really enjoyed it. Tips were great. So were the people I worked for, but it was a dead end job. I wasn't going any further." Jackson leaned forward. "I'm looking to invest my time in a career and company where I can advance."

"Tell me why I should hire you, other than the ability to make me laugh." Mr. Lloyd pushed out a hand. "Before you answer, I'll get right down to the nitty-gritty. If you have a problem working on a crew pounding a hammer to build and repair my billboards, or have fear of heights, this job isn't for you. Sometimes the crew is out on the road for weeks at a time in all kinds of weather. In other words, this entry level position is hard work and is not very glamorous. But there is plenty of room for advancement."

"Mr. Lloyd, braggadocian behavior isn't usually my manner, but you would be doing yourself a huge disservice if you didn't hire me. Honest to Pete, billboards have intrigued me ever since I was thirteen years old. I want you to teach me everything you know about billboards, from building the structures to selling their faces. In a reasonably short period of time, I'll be running this place." Jackson straightened his shoulders. "But never forgetting you are the boss. Start me at the bottom so I can climb my way to the top. As long as you are fair with me, sir, you will never find a more loyal and hard working employee."

"I don't see any college education on your application, but you have a way with words. My guess is you read a lot, correct?"

"Yes, sir," Jackson said. "I've always been a voracious reader. Growing up, besides playing on a baseball diamond, my other favorite place was the public library."

"I'm surprised an intelligent young man like you hasn't taken advantage of the GI Bill for school. Is there a reason why?"

Jackson nodded. A job killer of a question. How the hell was he supposed to answer?

"At one time I considered going to college full time after getting out of the service. Sometimes aspirations change due to unforeseen happenings. As it turned out, my going to school under the GI bill wasn't in the cards and I have no one to blame but myself."

"I have a host of other questions, Jackson, but I'm going to stop the interview process here. No use wasting your time and mine."

Lloyd placed the application on the desk, lifted the phone, and pushed a button. Jackson's heart fell as his stomach jumped. Did he ever have a chance for the job? Or did his last answer doom his fate? He wouldn't leave this office until those questions were answered.

"Rose, please cancel the rest of my interviews and bring in two cups of coffee." Mr. Lloyd extended his right hand to Jackson. "How soon can you start working for me?"

"I-I was ready as soon as I walked through the doorway, boss." Jackson shook hands to seal the deal, blew out a relieved breath, and reminded himself not to throw up.

"Let me clear up that perplexed look on your face, Jackson. I called your reference, Commander Thomas Oliver. He gave you a glowing report. He also informed me why you don't have the rights to a GI Bill, although your Other Than Honorable Discharge was changed to a General Discharge. The fact you didn't lie or alibi showed me great character. I would have punched out the asshole lieutenant too."

"Thank you, Mr. Lloyd. That means a lot to me."

"I've got a number of items to go over with you, but do you have any questions?"

"I've got a myriad of questions, Mr. Lloyd, starting with...would you have hired me if Rose had buzzed you only once when I was in the lobby?"

Mr. Lloyd laughed and slapped his leg again. "I think I'm going to learn as much from you as you are from me. Welcome aboard, Jackson. I'm hoping this is the start of something big for both of us."

Robert M. Davis

— PART TWO—

Robert M. Davis

CHAPTER THIRTEEN

JACKSON KING - 1994 CRACKERJACK OF THE YEAR was imprinted on a vinyl banner that stretched from one side of the banquet hall wall to the other like a high-priced billboard. Jackson sipped from his water glass and scanned the room packed full of prominent faces sitting at round tables. The who's who list included a multitude of business friends, competitors, the San Francisco Mayor, an ex-wife, and several other women he had slept with over the years.

Jackson's fingers searched the inside pocket of his tuxedo coat for a pack of Camel cigarettes, only to come back empty-handed. He had quit smoking over a year ago, but not yet mastered the habit of reaching. Another sip of water didn't calm him. Seeing his name in large letters made him feel like a tax evader at an IRS agent's convention.

A *San Francisco Chronicle* photographer kneeled in front of Jackson with her camera. He pushed a palm out towards her before she could snap another picture. She lowered the camera, rose to her feet, and pointed the lens at another table. His stomach rumbled the way it often did when he was on edge. The photographer was merely doing her job. On the flip side, she would have no way of understanding why he was camera shy.

Morgan Proffitt stepped up to the podium and tapped the microphone to determine if it was hot. *Thump, thump* sounded through the room's speakers. He nodded to Jackson who was seated at a table that included Jackson's executive assistant Rose, foreman Kenny, Proffitt's beautiful wife Helen, teenage daughter Katie, and account executive Virginia Wade - a budding star at Proffitt Advertising.

Jackson picked at a cuticle on his thumb; a habit he developed as a child and could never break. People often linked Jackson to Morgan Proffitt; a comparison Jackson appreciated while knowing the association was misguided. Jackson and Proffitt were in their middle forties and commanded successful advertising empires. They started at the bottom and worked their way to the top by being creative and tough, yet always fair. Plus they resided in the same affluent Seacliff neighborhood in San Francisco.

The comparisons end there. At six foot one, Proffitt stands a good three inches taller than Jackson. Proffitt's authoritative blue eyes make him movie star handsome. Most women find Jackson's dark chocolate brown eyes and mug alluring, even with the two inch scar line on his right cheek. Proffitt received his MBA from Stanford University. Jackson graduated cum laude in street smarts. Proffitt is happily married to his college sweetheart. Jackson is divorced and alone. Currently, his only relationship is an ongoing date with a psychiatrist who is determined to unwrap why, with all of his money and success, contentment continues to elude him.

"Good evening ladies and gentleman," Proffitt announced. "Welcome to the sixteenth annual Crackerjack of the Year banquet. My name is Morgan Proffitt, tonight's emcee. The Crackerjack Club consists of participating Northern California advertising agencies. The dictionary defines crackerjack as a person who shows marked ability or excellence at something. Each year our club honors one Crackerjack Club member with a miniature statue called The Jackie, an award that epitomizes outstanding achievement in the field of advertising, community involvement, and philanthropic endeavors. The Jackie couldn't be more aptly named for tonight's honoree, Jackson King, a man who is often referred to as The Sign King."

Proffitt placed his palm over the mic and cleared his throat. He stole a peek at his note cards lying on the lectern. The corner of his mouth lifted slightly.

"Our profession has been described by some as being populated by snakes and alligators. Others have referred to our line of work as being a close second to the world's oldest profession."

While Proffitt paused for the laughter to settle, Jackson eyed the round form of Richard Ransom, an adversary who epitomized Proffitt's well chosen words. Ransom's cutthroat tactics made him an enemy to J King Outdoor and other billboard companies. Jackson would have to deal with Ransom sooner rather than later. It was only a matter of how.

"For the majority of professionals in attendance those descriptions don't apply," Proffitt continued. "But make no mistake; advertising is a tough and competitive business. To survive, the men and women in this room have learned quickly they are *in* one day and *out* the next. It's nothing personal - at least most of the time - just an ad biz fact of life."

Jackson emitted a slight chuckle. Proffitt's depiction couldn't be more accurate. When Jackson lost an account, or an acquisition deal fell through, he was determined to keep those doors open and get them back. One client summed him up best by saying, "the only reason I'm signing this contract, King, you are one tenacious bastard and I prefer tenacious bastards." If a client had a problem or complaint, Jackson would resolve it at once, even if it was at his own expense. Many of his clients referred to Jackson as a good friend, yet all of their dealings had been over the phone.

"Before we present The Jackie trophy to the proprietor of J King Outdoor," Proffitt said, "I feel compelled to report we did a fair amount of digging into Jackson King's background. To set the record straight, here is what we discovered about who Jackson King really is."

Jackson's hand went to his stomach. The ulcer he had been nursing for years made its presence known. He ogled a squat glass with amber colored liquid sitting in front of Kenny. Jackson would trade one of his billboards located on the San Francisco skyway for a shot of Wild Turkey right now. How did Proffitt discover his name change secret?

"Jackson wasn't exactly cooperative when we requested his bio information," Proffitt said. "I feel confident in saying we know Jackson was born. It is where and when that is shadowed in mystery. Rumor has it, Jackson served in the navy after high school. When he was discharged, presumably honorably, Jackson worked several nondescript jobs before he was hired to construct and repair billboards for Lloyd Outdoor, a small Northern California billboard plant. In the process, Jackson learned how to lease land for future billboards. Then he would knock on potential advertiser doors to put a paying face on the newly built structures. It didn't take long for owner Andrew Lloyd to make Jackson the lease and sales manager, before becoming the General Manager.

"By the way," Proffitt held up a hand as if he was taking an oath, "this information came from my good friend Andrew Lloyd, not Jackson. Andrew loved Jackson like a son. So much so, Jackson inherited Lloyd Outdoor after Andrew passed away. Jackson changed the company name to J King Outdoor. With guile, guts, smarts, and determination, J King Outdoor has become one of the largest independently owned outdoor plants in the Western United States."

Moist heat attached to Jackson's cheeks and neck. He'd forever miss the paternal guidance from Andrew Lloyd, a man he affectionately called Boss. The boss left his business to Jackson because he earned it and Andrew knew Jackson would forever take care of Rose. What would Jackson's life be like if Andrew hadn't taken a chance on him?

Applause to something Morgan Proffitt had said brought Jackson back to present time. Every eye seemed focused on Jackson. How much longer would the ceremony last?

"It's no secret Jackson King keeps a very low profile," Proffitt said. "Believe me, it took a lot of prodding for Jackson to accept being the Crackerjack of the Year. What few people realize is how much Jackson has given back to the Bay Area community by providing food, clothes, and shelter for needy children, money for scholarships, and funding city park construction and reconstruction for play."

Proffitt smiled at Jackson and waited for another round of applause to die down. Jackson looked down at his shiny shoes, feeling conspicuous and undeserving. When he raised his eyes, Proffitt was pointing to the vinyl banner hanging on the wall.

"There are a host of people in this room who buy or sell outdoor space," Proffitt said. "The best copy on a fourteen by forty-eight foot display is seven words or less. With that rule in mind, our banner should have read: 'Jackson King - A Crackerjack in Life.' Without further ado, please welcome 1994's Crackerjack of the Year...Jackson King."

Jackson hurried to the podium to a thunderous applause. The sooner he got up there, said a few words including a sincere thank you, the faster the ordeal would be over. He cocked his head to the side and produced his signature grin; a mask that sometimes served as a shield. Proffitt handed him The Jackie, a shiny gold-plated figure holding a pen in one hand and briefcase in the other. The trophy was heavier than he expected.

Jackson stepped up to the podium, adjusted the microphone, and stared at Richard Ransom, the one person in the audience who wanted to either put him out of business or buy out J King Outdoor at an under valued price. Jackson didn't fear this man. On the contrary, Ransom would soon discover he was fucking with the wrong person.

CHAPTER FOURTEEN

Overhead lights affixed to the J King Outdoor building illuminated the front parking area as Jackson pulled his Mercedes into the space reserved with his name. After he popped open the trunk, he attached a leash to Yogi's collar, slid from the car, and lifted the small pound mutt he acquired nine months ago onto the cement.

With Yogi in tow trotting behind him, Jackson moved to the rear of his car. He puffed out a breath cloud. The early morning air was chilly, but not cold enough to produce a shiver. An explosion sounded. Yogi yelped. Jackson's shoulders were scrunched into his neck as he twisted around not knowing where the blast originated. It could have come from a tailpipe backfire, but it sounded more like a gunshot. No cars were in view. Nor could he see anyone in the darkness. Richard Ransom's face floated in his head. Jackson snatched The Jackie trophy from the trunk and took a second look around with the same results.

He unlocked the front door leading to the lobby. Yogi headed for his favorite spot underneath Jackson's office desk when Jackson unleashed him. He followed Yogi into the office, slid open the credenza door and deposited The Jackie inside with other awards.

After placing his suit coat on the back of his chair, Jackson sat down and rolled to the desk. Without using his hands, he maneuvered his black loafers off and set them near Yogi. He loosened his tie knot and freed the top button of his white dress shirt - all start the day routines he performed every morning unless he was on the road. He checked his date book organizer and prioritized a pile of pink phone message slips. Then he inspected the rest of his workplace decorated like a living room with a couch and easy chairs facing a coffee table. The sound system, TV, and video recorder were stationed on a cabinet. Various billboard photos - his first sold ad, eye-catching outdoor pictorial art, and creative slogans - adorned the walls. The one exception was an artist's characterization of hall of fame players from his stolen baseball card collection. He could still cite all of their statistics. Superman had his Fortress of Solitude, Jackson had his office.

Something heavy dropped to the floor in the reception area. It was too early for Rose and the staff to file in. He flashed on the explosion from a few minutes ago. Anyone spying on the business would recognize he left the front door unlocked for early arriving office employees and production crew.

Jackson grabbed his autographed Willie Mays bat and raced into the carpeted hall. As he rounded the corner leading to the lobby, he caught a glimpse of someone leaning against the reception desk as if it was holding her up. The petite brunette woman dressed in jeans, wrinkled red-patterned blouse, and high-top moccasins turned to him as his stocking feet hit the linoleum floor. He attempted to slow the impetus of his forward motion on the slick surface, but the bottom of his socks held no traction. The woman's eyebrows arched high as he skated past her and slammed into the wall to stop his momentum. The bat clattered to the floor along with Jackson. Stunned, he peered up at a face he didn't recognize. She made no attempt to help him up off the floor.

"Do you usually greet your visitors running at them with a baseball bat?" she asked.

"Sometimes I send Wolfgang, my Doberman Pinscher." Jackson got to his feet in stages and rubbed a sore elbow. There was no mistaking the accent; the lady was from West Virginia. "What brings you to J King Outdoor at this hour, miss...?"

"It's Mrs." She removed a tissue from a large black purse on the desk and dabbed her face with a shaky hand. "Mrs. Danielle Travers."

"Are you okay, Mrs. Travers?" Jackson asked in concerned tone.

"No, I'm not okay." She reached into her purse to reveal the handle of a revolver, and let it drop back into the bag. "I've never fired a gun at anyone before."

"That was you. You were shooting at me?"

"Actually, I was saving your bacon. I fired a warning shot at the two large hoods carrying tire irons, presumably to beat the crap out of you. They were hiding in the shadows of the vacant building across the street when you drove in. Lucky for you, I was waiting for your arrival from the factory next door. What are you, some kind of mob guy?"

"I've been called many things before, but never a mobster. I have a good idea who sent them." He touched the scar on his cheek. "Thank you, Mrs. Travers. I owe you one."

"I prefer Dani to Mrs. Travers."

Jackson studied her face again. Obviously, she didn't come here to dazzle him. Her clothes looked like she had slept in them. Her dark blue eyes set off attractive features un-enhanced by makeup, not even lipstick. She was either self-confident or she didn't give a damn about her appearance. He noticed a suitcase next to the desk side.

"And you were waiting for me because..."

"Well, it wasn't for employment, although I am presently unemployed. I'm an artist and art instructor. I left West Virginia to find you, Jackson King."

"I'm sorry," he said. "You have probably mistaken me for someone else. It's not the first time that has happened. King is a fairly common last name."

"But Kingman isn't." She combed her short hair with a hand.

Jackson's stomach jumped. Conversely, Dani was able to manage her nerves. This was one hell of a way to start a Monday or any other freakin' day.

"My staff and crew will be filing through here soon. Let's talk in a more private place."

Jackson lifted the suitcase and handed Dani her purse that was almost as heavy. She followed him into his office and sat in a chair across from the couch. Her eyes narrowed when he shut the door.

"Would you please leave the door open, Jackson."

Jackson reopened the door, deposited the suitcase by the chair's arm, and sat down on the couch. He had no idea who or what brought her to him. Was she here to hustle him? It wouldn't be the first time. Most likely she knows the tale of his mother killing his father. Is that what this was all about? Maybe she was an artist - a con artist. Or she could be a reporter posing as an artist to do an expose rehashing one of the biggest murder stories in the state's history. He went to his desk and brought her a pad of paper and a pencil.

"Would you please draw something for me?" he asked.

"I get it. My art ability or inability is like a lie detector test. Smart move, Jackson. By the way, whatever happened to your West Virginia accent?"

"I gave it to a wonderful woman; a speech therapist who also doubled as a librarian."

Dani shot Jackson a curious look before the pencil in her hand moved as if it had a mind of its own. In minutes she handed him a depiction of a billboard and a man in overalls standing on the cat-walk with a paint brush.

"Very impressive," he said. "I now know you are an artist and missing person locator. I'm assuming you didn't go to all of your trouble to find me so you can promote your art talent. Let's skip past pleasantries to get straight to the point. What do you want, Dani? You seem to know me or about me, but I have no recollection of you."

"We've never met before. However, we did attend a primary school at the same time in West Virginia. You won the junior high spelling contest before your family moved to another town. I was the third grade spelling champ. At the same assembly, I also won a blue ribbon for a drawing. It took me a long time, at great expense, to track you down."

"How did you find me?" Jackson picked at a cuticle.

"It wasn't easy, but I knew your family relocated to Reno, Nevada."

"Sorry, but that is absolute bullshit. We never told anyone where we were going."

"Oh, but you did." Her expressive blue eyes widened.

"Is your maiden name Peppers?" he asked in a stern voice.

"My maiden name was Williams. Look Jackson, I'm aware of what people have said about your mother murdering your father and getting away with it. And the mysterious death of your two uncles in a coal mine cave-in. Most folks believe it was no accident."

"I didn't even know my uncles were dead," he said. "How long ago was the cave in?"

"Maybe fifteen years. When I was in Reno trying to find you, I learned your brother had died from congenital heart failure while you were in the service. Soon after, your mother passed. I'm sorry. Tragedy follows you like a shadow."

Jackson was breathing hard through his nose. Dani's presence was like waking up from a bad dream and finding it wasn't a dream. How much crazier was this going to get?

"Why did you track me down, Dani?"

"Dalton Peppers said your family moved to Reno. It took me days to find someone there who knew you. I convinced a grocer, Mr. Ornstein, to tell me where you relocated."

"You must have been very convincing for Mr. O to break his oath," Jackson said. "How do you know Dalton Peppers? And what do you want from me?"

"It's probably not what you are thinking. We have something else in common besides being good spellers. My stepbrother, Dalton Peppers, repeatedly raped me as a child and took something I cherished most. Does that ring any bells, Jackson? I want you to help me find Dalton."

"Why would you ever want to see Dalton again?" he asked.

"To kill him!"

CHAPTER FIFTEEN

Unabashed tears formed in Jackson's eyes; for this poor woman - for himself. He understood why Dani wanted to kill Dalton Peppers, although it shocked him to hear those words from her. Dani's lips were clenched; a hard look that belied her pleasant features. He had seen the expression many times before in a mirror when his thoughts turned to that morning in the motel shower with Dalton Peppers.

Jackson went to the door, pulled the knob towards him, leaving it ajar for Dani. He positioned himself on the couch to create a direct sightline to her. Yogi appeared from underneath the desk and trotted straight to Dani. How strange? The only person his dog usually warmed up to was Jackson. Yogi stood on his hind legs and pressed his tiny paws against her knees. Dani lifted him onto her lap.

"Words can't undo what that monster did to you, Dani. But I'm sincerely sorry."

She responded with a nod. Her right hand kept twisting the wedding band on her finger until Yogi pawed for her attention. A few loving neck scratches made him turn over on his back for a tummy rub. A hint of a smile came to Dani's lips. She seemed more at ease. Animals have a keen sense about humans. The fickle dog Jackson saved from being euthanized at the pound may have found his soul master.

Jackson leaned back into the couch. Violated is violated, in spite of the size of one's moccasins. If Yogi could eliminate a few seconds of shame, guilt, and depression Dani endured every day of her life after being molested by Dalton, Jackson was all for sharing.

"If you don't want to talk about it, I certainly understand." Jackson leaned his forearms into his thighs and folded his hands. "Were you sincere about wanting to kill Dalton?"

"Oh, I was sincere, Jackson. But I could never actually go through with the act of killing anyone. Sure would like to give him the impression he was a goner, though. You can't look me in the eye and tell me you haven't thought about killing Dalton Peppers."

"Marie, my therapist, made me realize resentment left to marinate often becomes a flavor enhancer called payback. As appealing as it sounds, I've learned through therapy that revenge isn't the answer. Instead, it's much healthier to unburden one's soul by verbally releasing festering poison inside. Sounds like a bunch of crap, but she's right. To answer your question, I've thought about eliminating Dalton Peppers many times."

"At least you can afford to pay for a shrink," she said. "Has it really helped you?"

"A very good question." Jackson crossed his legs. "I think so, but it's a long process. By getting me to open up, Marie has helped put meaning to things I've never understood before, which can be beneficial as well as painful."

"I've never talked about what Dalton did to me with anyone, including my mother."

"Let me guess," Jackson said. "Dalton promised you he would first kill your mother then you if you ever said anything. And you believed him."

"Yes, how did you know? Oh, of course... Dalton must have said the same thing to you."

A chill ran through Jackson's body after he recalled Dalton's threat. It wasn't Dalton's words that made him shiver. It was Dalton's menacing tone of anticipated pleasure to inflict the same kind of pain on his brother and mother.

"You indicated having a husband, Dani? You must have shared with him—"

"My husband and I have been legally separated for many years. We never bothered to get a divorce. From the beginning, I realized it was a mistake. We weren't together very long; two months. We worked at the same place and were friends. One day he asked me to marry him. I never dated much. I thought, maybe being married would help me. I couldn't bring myself to tell him what Dalton did to me as a child. I was too ashamed. The nightmares never went away. Nor did waking up in a sweat or feeling fear. He started calling me

Dani-freeze." She glanced at her left hand. "Don't get me wrong. He's really a good guy, but totally incapable of dealing with a woman like me. What man would be capable? He has a lady friend now. I hope they get married. Then I'll know I didn't ruin him." She cocked her head to the side. "Did you ever marry, Jackson?"

"Oh, yeah. My ex put up with my drinking and womanizing for a long time since I was, and continue to be, a good provider. I'm also a workaholic. Conquering two out of three ain't bad. I can't see where I'd ever give up being obsessive about my work. Believe it or not, I was an improvement compared to her father. She's a great gal. We get along fine."

"I thought marriage would make it easier to get over what Dalton did to me. How ignorant could I be? The wedding ring on my finger is to keep men at bay."

Jackson peered down at the plush office carpet. Obviously, what Dalton did to them was a common thread to why their marriages failed. But they grew up responding in different ways. Marie made him realize he had a need to jump into bed with any willing woman as a way to prove his heterosexuality. Dani went in another direction.

"At what age did Dalton violate you?" he asked.

"It started with touching." Yogi's eyes were closed as Dani massaged his chest and stomach. "I was six years old. Dalton called it a game. Before long it escalated into rape and it didn't stop until he left town with your family."

"You were only six, Dani. Big difference. I knew it was wrong, but I didn't fight back. How did you find out what Dalton did to me? Did he go back to West Virginia?"

"Not to my knowledge," she said. "Dalton left our home to travel with your family. Two days after he left, he called the house. I was home alone when he called. He told me what state he was in, but I don't remember. It scared me to hear his voice. I thought he was coming back. He told me how much he enjoyed what he did to you and stealing your baseball trading cards. I wasn't even nine years old. What I will never forget is how euphoric he was after molesting you. He told me not to forget him - some day he would be back for more. Years later I realized the things he took from us had equal value to him. I have often wondered how many duffle bags it took to satisfy the sick son of a bitch."

Every time Jackson saw someone with a green duffle bag, his heart started to beat like a war drum. Dani had been right about how Dalton valued what he stole. What possession of Dani's did Dalton put in the duffle bag?

"I just realized something," Dani said. "By leaving West Virginia, your family saved me. I'm grateful, but sorry you had to be Dalton's next victim. Tell me why your baseball cards were so dear to you?"

"We moved so often I had to make new friends at each stop. It wasn't always easy - the Kingman name became synonymous with scorn. My baseball cards were my companions. My escape." He touched the scar on his cheek. "What made you think I could help you find Dalton?"

"Well, Mr. Crackerjack, based on Sunday's San Francisco Chronicle article, you are a rich, compassionate, and charitable man who helps people in need; a good Samaritan. I was hoping you knew where Dalton was located."

"You can't believe everything you read in newspapers," he said. "They tend to over-inflate someone to make an article newsworthy. I don't have a clue where Dalton is."

"False modesty on your part? Or do you have a problem accepting compliments?" She flicked a hand. "Doesn't matter. From your shocked expression when I said I wanted to kill Dalton, I assumed you didn't go after him. Why?"

"A question I've asked myself many times. If I came face to face with Dalton again, I'm unsure what I'd do. Would I forgive him? Or would I avenge what he did to me?"

"I'm not looking for revenge," she said. "I'm looking for closure. Fear he instilled in me has never left. It gets worse each day. If I can confront him on my terms, maybe the fear will vanish so I can close my eyes, get a full night's sleep, and wake up feeling safe."

"How do you even know Dalton is still alive?" he asked.

"I don't. But with your help, maybe we can find the answer to that question."

The phone buzzed. Jackson walked to his desk and pressed a button.

"Yes, Rose," Jackson said, without lifting the receiver.

"Kenny is on line one. He's out in the field. He says it's imperative he speak to you."

"Thank you, Rose. I'm in conference right now, but I'll take Kenny's call. Would you please bring in a carafe of hot coffee and anything eatable?"

"The coffee's brewing as we speak," Rose answered.

"Excuse me, Dani." Jackson picked up the receiver. "Good morning, Kenny."

"It's not a good morning, Jackson," Kenny said in an edgy tone. "Two more of our boards were vandalized. This isn't some kid with a graffiti fetish. We're dealing with a dirt bag's major vendetta against us. The same hypocrite who attended your crackerjack affair and applauded you with a shit-eating grin knowing full well what was in store for us. Maybe you should call your police commissioner buddy. Or better yet, I know a guy who can make Richard Ransom permanently disappear. Just say the word, Jackson."

Jackson's gut said hello. Kenny's work ethic was similar to Jackson's. The six foot five inch two hundred and sixty pound foreman took the vandalism as a personal affront, but they didn't always deal with issues in the same way.

"You know I don't operate that way, Kenny. But enough is enough. We need to put an end to the sabotage ASAP. It's costing us a fortune."

Dani's curious stare caught Jackson's eye. Yogi's snore caught his ear. J King Outdoor was closing in on Richard Ransom's Double R Outdoor as the leading independent billboard plant in the western United States. The growth of Jackson's business inspired Ransom to perform more acts like chopping down trees in the middle of the night that blocked the view of his billboards, building new structures without permits, using illegal extensions, bad-mouthing J King to potential advertisers, and vandalizing the structures of competing billboard plants. Ransom was more than willing to pay heavy fines and lawyer fees to keep him out of jail for his malicious deeds. Jackson had a snippet of an idea of how to stop Ransom, but not a hint of how to implement the plan.

"There's something else you should know," Kenny said. "Nancy, the graphic artist Ransom stole away from us with an offer doubling her wages quit Double R Outdoor. He badgered her for inside J King information as well as hitting on her for sex."

Jackson gripped his letter opener as if it was a knife. His womanizing days had cost him a wife and a ton of money, but he never once fooled around with any of his employees. Marie, his shrink, explained the cause of his need to seduce women; a reason that should never be mistaken as an excuse. He had not had sex, alcohol, or a cigarette since he started seeing Dr. Stiller over a year ago.

"Obviously, Ransom didn't hire Nancy for her artistic talents. I didn't blame her for taking Ransom's offer. She has two kids and a husband on disability. Tell Nancy to come in and see me. We'll work something out. Thanks for the heads-up, Kenny." Jackson glanced at Dani. "I've got a plan floating in my brain on how to take down Ransom."

"Sorry about the interruption, Dani." Jackson sat on the couch again.

"Knock, Knock." Rose's shoulder pushed the door. "I have coffee and Monday morning happy bagels." She put the tray on the coffee table. "Is there anything else, Jackson?"

"Rose, this is Mrs. Danielle Travers." Jackson removed a credit card from his wallet and handed it to Rose. "Would you please get Mrs. Travers a room at the Fairmont Hotel?"

Rose questioned Jackson with a cold-eyed stare before leaving. Was she thinking his vow of abstinence for the past year was about to be broken? Rose had been Andrew Lloyd's secretary and mistress when Jackson was first hired. The loyalty bond between them was stronger than the coffee she had been serving Andrew and Jackson for over forty years.

"I have literally spent every dollar I have to find you." Dani stood, gently placed Yogi on the chair, and moved to stand in front of Jackson. "My credit cards are maxed. I have no one else to turn to. For the love of God, Jackson, will you please help me find Dalton?"

Jackson took her hand and guided Dani to sit beside him on the couch. She didn't remove her fingers. They stared at each other. Did she feel safe with him? Or was Dani enduring their intimacy as a way to get something she wanted? Jackson was about to do the same to her. He now needed Dani as much as she needed him. Whether she was aware of it or not, she could trust him. But could he trust her? Were there really two guys with tire irons about to attack him? Or was that a figment of this woman's creative imagination?

"I'm sorry, Dani," Jackson said. "I can't help you..."

Dani removed her fingers from Jackson's hand. "So it was simply lip service when you said you owed me a favor."

"On the contrary, I honor all of my promises. When I said I can't help you, you didn't let me finish. As you probably could tell from my phone conversation, I have a pressing business problem that needs my immediate attention. It impacts over a hundred of my employees and independent contractors. So let's make a deal."

She flinched back. "What kind of deal?"

"You can be a godsend to me and my company. I need another favor."

"What kind of favor?" she asked. "How is it possible I could be useful to your company? And, finally, what do I get in return?"

Jackson smiled. Questions he would have asked in a business negotiation. She was sharp. More than ever, he was convinced Dani was the missing component to his plan of attack.

"When was the last time you wore makeup, a tight skirt, and a low cut blouse?" he asked.

Dani slapped Jackson's face.

CHAPTER SIXTEEN

D r. Marie Stiller held up a *San Francisco Chronicle* newspaper clipping that included an attached photo. Jackson rolled his eyes. He leaned forward on the green psychiatrist couch, uncrossed his legs, and planted both shoes onto the floor. She began to read the article out loud until he waved both hands for her to stop.

"I usually reserve my agenda items for the end of a session, but I'm making an exception today." Marie jiggled the article. "Were you ever going to tell me about your Crackerjack of the Year award? This is quite an honor, Jackson."

"Marie, you know damn well why I wouldn't say anything. I didn't deserve the award."

"That, of course, is your Imposter Phenomenon kicking in, Jackson. You remember, we have talked about this psych syndrome before, based on your secret feelings of fraudulence. So when you say you don't deserve the award - that comes from your belief you are a phony and fearful someone will discover your big secret. It is also a motivator that makes you work harder and overachieve."

He didn't always agree with Marie, but she had been a life-saving blessing to him. She placed the article on the table next to her easy chair and held up an old photo of an emaciated blonde woman.

"If a ninety-eight pound anorexic female looks at her image in a mirror and tells you she is fat, what would you say to her, Jackson?"

"I get the analogy, Marie. But it doesn't change the way we view ourselves."

"Correct," she said. "We need to change that mindset and retrain your thinking. How about if you learn how to accept a compliment or praise by responding with two powerful words: *thank you*. That's it. You condition yourself to respond with a simple *thank you* until it becomes a good habit, rather than deflecting or rejecting what is said."

"*Thank you*, Dr. Stiller." Jackson offered her a mock smile.

"Your conditioning has made me a man who doesn't smoke, drink, or chase women anymore. Good thing I was already house broken before you became my therapist. Hell, I'm so dull now I order vanilla at Baskin-Robbins. Seriously, I can't remember a time in my life when I was able to accept any form of compliment, so your record of accomplishments with me will probably get tarnished with your latest request."

Marie held the picture of the blonde out further for Jackson to get a better look. He squinted at the photo, unable to understand the connection.

"Instead of the chubby, gray haired woman sitting before you, this is what I looked like before I got help. It took awhile, but now I can thoroughly enjoy two scoops of vanilla coated with a hot chocolate topping on a sugar cone and not feel guilty. So I'm living proof it can be done. I believe, in time, you can condition yourself to overcome part or all of the Imposter Phenomenon too." Marie removed her glasses. "Now, what's new with you, Jackson, besides being the Crackerjack of the Year?"

He leaned back into the couch and detailed the serious problem he was having with competitor Richard Ransom and the advent of a mystifying lady who appeared at his office yesterday morning saying she also had been molested by Dalton Peppers as a child.

"Do you really believe this woman who appeared out of nowhere scared two hoods away from you by firing her gun? Or this Ransom guy sent them?"

"Not for a fact, but my gut says yes to both questions," he said. "I heard the shot, but didn't see the attackers. Dani showed me a pistol she carries in her purse."

"You have shared moments in your life where you have lost your temper as a child, in your teens and as an adult. I recall you telling me when you were a catcher in a youth baseball game, you physically attacked a mouthy batter who was badgering you about the shooting of your father. Or the time you punched out a navy lieutenant. How did you react after Dani slapped your face?"

"I was sorry I wasn't wearing a catcher's mask." He rubbed his cheek. "To this day, I have no regrets about pounding on Pete Long. But I learned a very valuable lessen from pummeling the lieutenant;

it cost me my GI Bill. So to answer your question, when Dani slapped me, I apologized for not approaching her in a different way. She had every right to hit me. I gripped her hand so as not to get slugged again and explained how she was the perfect person to help me with my Richard Ransom troubles."

"Before we discuss the Richard Ransom operation, how do you feel about Dani finding you and exposing your past?"

"Conflicted. I was furious. What right did this lady or anyone have to hunt me down and bring out memories I chose to bury. Subsequently, I realized it wasn't about me. It was about Dani desperately trying to chase the ghost that has been haunting her all these years. Honestly, commiserating with someone who suffered the same indignities was a good thing. What I went through was nothing like what Dani had to endure. My anger towards Dalton Peppers came raging back because of what he did to her."

"You just met this woman, Jackson. Do you have feelings for her?"

"It wouldn't matter if I did, Marie. Dani was upfront about her history of not desiring a romantic relationship - the effects of what Dalton did to her as a child. I will respect those boundaries." He smiled. "Dani kind of reminds me of myself in how tenacious she was in finding me. She's smart, talented, and gutsy. I loved hearing her West Virginia accent. Yeah, I like Dani. And I would like to make her hurt go away."

"Let's talk about how you want to use Dani in your Richard Ransom scheme? I don't get the tie in."

"Ransom's graphic artist, Nancy, worked for me before he hired her away. She quit after Ransom tried to get inside information about my company. He also hit on her for sex. The man is a hall of fame scuzzbag."

"What does any of this have to do with Dani?"

"Dani is an accomplished artist and art instructor. She is an attractive woman, but she downplays her looks. With a dab of makeup, she'd be a knockout. If Dani cold-called Double R Outdoor looking for employment, Ransom would probably suspect it was more than a coincidence and I had sent her to him. He'd verify his suspicions by doing a background check on Dani. What he would discover is Dani has lived in West Virginia her whole life and is a well respected graphic artist. She actually moonlighted for an ad agency in West Virginia doing billboard and ad campaign creative to supplement her income."

"So you want Dani to be *your* inside spy, inspired by Ransom himself."

"That's one way of putting it," Jackson said. "All I need Dani to do is find out when and where Ransom's next billboard vandalism will take place. If she can obtain that information in advance, we could give my police connections a heads up and catch Ransom's goons in the act."

"Wouldn't Ransom ask why Dani is in the San Francisco Bay Area looking for work?"

"You're good, Marie. The storyline for Dani is she relocated to San Francisco to live with an aunt after separating from her husband. She chose Double R Outdoor first because they had the largest ad in the yellow pages. She's planning to apply at other outdoor and advertising agencies in the area, but money is tight and she really needs a job as soon as possible. It's a perfect cover and entirely plausible."

"Aren't you concerned about putting Dani in physical and psychological peril?"

"Of course I am, Marie. I didn't sugarcoat anything. I explained to Dani why Nancy left her job at Double R Outdoor. I've also told her how Ransom is trying to put all of his competitors, especially me, out of business one way or another. Dani is no fool. She fully understood I would be of no use to her until my Ransom problem is resolved. I likened Ransom to Dalton Peppers. They both violate people to get what they want."

"Good line, Jackson, comparing Ransom to Dalton. Did Dani accept the assignment of being your mole?"

"Not exactly," he said. "We negotiated a deal."

"What kind of deal?"

"Dani is willing to take a risk because she needs me to help her. Don't forget, she carries a gun. Also, Dani didn't have a cell phone, so I loaned her a company phone. If she finds herself in trouble, all she has to do is hit one number. My foreman Kenny will have a few *friends* on ready alert minutes away. If anyone can get Ransom's trust, it's Dani.

"What deal did you make with Dani, Jackson?" Marie notched up her volume.

"In return for taking part in the scheme to nail Ransom, I will hire a private investigator to find Dalton Peppers. If the PI discovers Dalton is alive, we will confront him together." Jackson held up a hand. "There's more. If we find any clues leading to the possessions Dalton stole from us, I'm obligated to follow the trail to its end."

"What did Dalton take from Dani?" Marie asked.

"She didn't volunteer that information and I didn't ask. I doubt it was baseball cards, but it must be something valuable for her to go to all of this trouble."

Marie chewed on the end of her glasses. Jackson knew from experience she was contemplating a delicate question.

"How do you feel about pursuing Dalton Peppers after all these years?" she asked.

"When I make a deal, Marie, I honor it."

"It's one of your many redeeming qualities, Jackson."

"Hardly a redeeming quality...never mind. *Thank you, Dr. Stiller.* Are you saying it wouldn't be prudent for me to agree to seek the whereabouts of Dalton Peppers? In other words, I shouldn't have made that deal with Dani."

"I can see how searching for and confronting Dalton could prove beneficial to both of you, as long as you are there for the right reasons. However, if the purpose is to do bodily harm to Dalton, I strongly advise you to void your contract."

"I can't speak for Dani, but I'm rational about our deal. The chance of our finding Dalton Peppers is incredibly low. Even if we locate Dalton, the odds of recovering my baseball card collection are a hundred times worse. I use a private detective from time to time. If Whitey can't find Dalton, no one can. Nor would it surprise me to learn Dalton is dead, maybe by the hands of someone he violated. Or maybe he changed his name, making it impossible to find him. Hell, he could even be living in another country."

"What if, by some strange quirk of fate, you find Dalton alive and he's the same contemptible person?" Marie tapped her pen against the pad. "Or what if he's worse?"

Jackson stared at the bookcase. "How could Dalton Peppers be worse? Look, there are a lot of unknowns. I can't swear Dani is trustworthy. Yet, for some reason, I have a powerful urge to help her. That, more than anything, is the reason I agreed to her conditions. Maybe our joining forces could be the best medicine for both of us."

"You are a wealthy man, Jackson. Perhaps you should consider playing part of this equation another way. How do you feel about offering to buy Dani whatever possession Dalton stole from her? Same goes for you. Purchase every baseball card, including the Henry Wagner card you talk about, until your collection is whole again. You could even buy old cigar boxes to house them in. It could be an enjoyable, productive project and it wouldn't cost you anywhere near the time, money, and frustration following lost trails to your possessions."

"Sentimentally, it wouldn't be the same," he said. "I loved each and every one of those cards as if they were alive. Secondly, you may be good at psychological mumbo-jumbo, but your math is way off. The Honus Wagner - not Henry Wagner - American Tobacco baseball card at today's 1994 value is worth close to a million dollars. My 1951 Bowman Mickey Mantle rookie card goes for hundreds of thousands. My Ty Cobb card is worth—"

"My goodness." Her pen dropped. "Do you think Dalton realized he pilfered a fortune?"

"Baseball cards held no monetary value back then. I don't think Dalton was much of a baseball fan. For all I know, he may have thrown the cards away."

Marie glanced at the clock residing in a bookcase.

"In the time we have left, have you thought about why Dalton would take belongings prized by the people he violated?"

"Because he is a mean, sadistic bastard."

"I certainly don't disagree, but it could be there is more to it than that. What if the possessions were as valuable to him in a different way? What if each item triggered lusty memories of the individuals he sullied?"

Jackson picked at a cuticle. Right or wrong, Marie cracked open a door his mind had closed —access to hope.

"If your last theory holds true, Dalton could still have my baseball cards."

"Wouldn't that be a dream come true." Marie stood. "Our time is up, Jackson. It appears you may have a challenging week ahead of you. Please don't hesitate to call me if you need my assistance. And congratulations again for being Crackerjack of the Year."

"Thank you, Dr. Stiller."

CHAPTER SEVENTEEN

Jackson knocked on the front door of Rose's Millbrae house, something he had done hundreds of times before. This time his presence in the neighboring San Francisco city was more business than social. His knuckles curled to knock again, then straightened after a scraping metal latch was released from guard duty and the door swung open.

"Wow!" Jackson blinked twice when he caught a full view of Dani. What a difference from when they met two days ago in his office. "Wow!"

"I know." Dani peered down at her black business skirt outfit. "Rose applied my makeup before I met with Mr. Ransom today. It felt like I was a different person wearing a mask. Don't I look ridiculous? I was going to change, but Rose insisted I wait for you."

"No offense, Dani," Jackson said, as he moved past her and entered the house. "But if ridiculous means stunning, yes you look incredibly ridiculous, blonde wig and all."

Dani didn't respond. Yogi skidded to a stop on the slick floor in front of Jackson. After an exchange of wet kisses for several furry neck massages, they moved into a kitchen connecting to a family room. The contents of two pots bubbled on stove burners. Rose left the salad she was building to give Jackson a hug. Then she handed him a tray with a pitcher of lemonade and two glasses.

"You two go out to the patio while I finish up," Rose said, lifting her wine glass.

"Rose insisted I stay with her rather than at the Fairmont," Dani said. "She made me feel like family after one night. The only problem, she won't let me help her."

"Rose never lets anyone assist in her kitchen," he said. "In my case, that's a good thing."

Jackson carried the tray out to the patio and set it on a bar-beque table. The sun had not quite set. They sat on benches facing each other while Yogi wondered off to sniff every backyard bush, tree, and flower. Dani filled both glasses and handed one to Jackson. His stomach growled, but not from hunger. He was anxious to hear about Dani's job interview with Double R Outdoor. Her expression and demeanor gave nothing away.

"How did the interview go today?" Jackson traced the scar on his cheek with a thumb. "Did he hire you?"

Damn. His words came out anxious; a tell he often spotted in others.

"Before I get to the interview," Dani said, "I want you to know how grateful I am for the clothes and cosmetics. I'm sure Rose enjoyed spending your money much more than I did. And I especially appreciate your loaning me Yogi while I'm here."

"The interview, Dani..." His stomach traveled past queasy and into upset.

"I'm sorry, Jackson. I know how important the Ransom issue is to you. I should have called instead of waiting for you to meet with us. Mr. Ransom was impressed with my resume and skills as a graphic artist. He made me wait in a conference room while he verified my West Virginia references and confirmed I'm currently living with my *Aunt Rose*. When he returned, he hired me on the spot. I start tomorrow morning."

"Well done, Dani." Jackson threw a celebratory fist in the air. "I knew you could do it."

A raging river of adrenaline surged through Jackson's veins. Dani was smiling, but her blue eyes didn't convey an invitation for a celebratory hug. Would she ever be able to trust a man again?

"Jackson, there's no guarantee I'll be able to get the information you are after."

"I don't expect any guarantees," he said. "But if anyone can pull this off, it's you, Dani."

"You really know how to pressure a gal. Rose told me you are the most honorable person she has ever met. That you saved her in more ways than one when Mr. Lloyd died. I hope you don't make her out to be a liar." Dani exhaled a deep breath. "Are you going to renege on our deal if I don't get what you want from Ransom?"

"I won't break our agreement. Instead, I can offer you an amendment."

"No way. A deal is deal." She placed both hand on her hips. "You can't back out now."

"The stipulation isn't about *me*. It's for *you*. You have proved yourself to me, Dani. In doing so, I've also put you in a very precarious position. So I'm adding an opt-out provision for *you* to cancel our agreement at any time."

"What's the catch, Jackson?" Dani asked in a defiant tone. "After the small fortune you invested in me, why would you offer a way for me to opt out?" She made a snapping sound with her fingers. "Of course, by making it easier for me to walk away, you won't have to uphold your end of the deal? As far as I'm concerned, bubba, our agreement is set in superglue and your revision isn't necessary."

"I've never had to work so hard to be fair." Jackson pulled a cell phone and address book from his pocket. "The amendment is there if you change your mind."

Jackson punched in a series of numbers on the cell phone. George White's recorded voice came on, followed by the annoying beep.

"Whitey, this is Jackson King. I have a job only the best private investigator in Northern California can handle." Jackson winked at Dani. "I want you to find a person from my past. His name is Dalton Peppers. I don't know if he has a middle name. The last time I saw him was in the state of Kansas over thirty years ago. At that time, he was traveling with my family on his way to the Sacramento area in California to work as a mechanic in his uncle's garage. He was about five feet eleven inches tall. No distinguishing scars, but he has two different colored eyes - one brown and one bluish grey. Dalton should now be in his fifties. Please call me on my cell phone after you receive this message."

Jackson replaced the cell phone and address book back into his pocket. Part of his promise to Dani had been launched. He didn't expect Whitey to find Dalton Peppers or maybe even take the case. But Dani's eyes danced with pleasure.

"There is one thing you will never have to worry about, Dani," Jackson said. "When I make an agreement, I honor it."

"I'm the same way, Jackson." She sipped her lemonade. "Another thing we have in common."

"Five minutes before dinner's ready," Rose shouted.

Dani stood. She lost two inches of height by stepping out of her new high heel shoes and removed the blonde wig.

"If you will excuse me, I think I'll change and wipe off the makeup before we eat."

"Wait," Jackson said. "If the private investigator asks me what Dalton Peppers stole from you, what should I tell him?"

"Tell him my mother left my daddy because he was a poor coal miner who didn't make near enough money to satisfy her. She ended up with Dalton's father, a traveling tractor salesman. Before my daddy died from lung disease, he went out and bought two very expensive frames. One of the frames was for my spelling champion certificate. The other frame was for a first place blue ribbon I won with a crayon drawing." Dani's voice quivered. "My daddy was so proud of me. No amount of money can replace that sentiment.

"Dalton knew how much I loved my daddy and the frames he bought. I desperately want those frames Dalton stole from me. There's more, Jackson. I also want to return all the irreplaceable valuables Dalton took from the other children he violated. And finally," tears laced with mascara lined her cheeks, "I need to know for sure Dalton can't molest me or another child ever again. I don't intend to kill Dalton. But if pointing a gun at him is the only way I can accomplish my mission, then so be it."

Jackson gave Dani a sympathetic nod. If Whitey failed to find Dalton they would have no chance of recovering their possessions. How much more disappointment could this lady take?

CHAPTER EIGHTEEN

Jackson ran a finger down an inventory spreadsheet page attempting to predict which one of his billboards Richard Ransom would vandalize next. If there was a pattern, so far he was unable to catch it. He lifted his head and stared at a billboard photo hanging on the wall. Maybe he was overthinking Ransom's methodology. What if Ransom's system was to pin a J King inventory list on a dartboard and wherever the dart point landed was the next structure to be damaged?

He flipped to the following page. A weeks worth of infiltrating Dani as a spy inside Double R Outdoor wasn't working any better. Dani's eyes and ears had not produced one smidgen of helpful feedback. Setting Ransom up to hire Dani had seemed like an ideal way to catch the son of a bitch at his own game.

What if Ransom knew Dani was Jackson's spy? In that case, it would be smart to feed her with false clues, but Dani had received nothing. What if Ransom had sent Dani to J King Outdoor in the first place? That would make Dani a double agent. He shook his head, trying to rid the crazy thoughts. Or were they crazy thoughts?

Yogi snuggled against Jackson's stocking foot. He missed his little buddy at night, but it was love at first scratch for both Dani and Yogi. Rose brought Yogi to the office each morning so Jackson could have some doggie time.

"Knock, knock." Rose stood in the open doorway with coffee cups in her hands.

"Jackson, can you spare a few minutes?"

Before he could answer, Rose entered the office and delivered a steaming cup to him. She settled into one of the chairs fronting his desk. Jackson pushed the printouts aside, sipped his coffee, and waited for Rose to open a conversation he most likely didn't want to have. The hat he wore as boss became invisible when Rose needed a sit down. Her squinty-eyed scowl and taut smile could be construed as a smowl, not a word he could ever find in the diction-ary. He visualized Rose's expression on a billboard ad with "Beware of the Smowl."

"I think it was really sweet of you to share Yogi with Dani," Rose said.

"Being sweet had nothing to do with it...*thank you, Rose*. It wasn't hard to see Yogi's heart belongs to Dani. But you didn't come in here to talk about that, did you?"

"After all the many years of our working together, I can't put anything past you, can I?" Rose's sarcasm brought a smile to both of their faces. "Your buddy Fred Aldred called earlier when you were on the other line. One of his Bourbon Hill billboards in the Chico/Paradise area was vandalized last night. He thinks it's another Ransom hit job and wants to compare notes with you."

"I'll call Fred when we're done. He's always a good person to brainstorm with. What else do you have?"

"The fortune teller client who paid you up front in cash on a year contract for the Hayward board called with a request to slightly amend the agreement she signed with you. She wants her sister's name on the contract to replace her name. That's a new one on me, Jackson."

"She's in a big divorce battle with a deadbeat husband," Jackson said. "You would think if she was a seer, she would have known what a louse her husband was going to be." He waited for Rose to stop laughing. "She's trying to hide assets from him. I'll call her when I get a chance. Now, why are you really here?"

"Are you aware you haven't spent this much time at my house since Andrew died?" Rose said. "Don't get me wrong, Jackson. I never could have gotten over Andrew's passing without you. I love your visits. For me, it has been like a week's worth of Thanksgiving." She gazed at her coffee cup. "You carried Andrew for several years and now you are carrying me, for which I am forever grateful. In many ways you and I are a lot alike. Neither one of us will get voted Saint of the Year for past behavior. I was never proud about being Andrew's lover, but I wouldn't change our time together for anything."

"Where are you going with this, Rose?" The cream in the coffee didn't soothe his stomach.

"Your presence at my house isn't about me or Yogi. Or for Dani's covert assignment to nail Richard Ransom. Or for chasing after the whereabouts of Dalton Peppers." She placed her cup on the desk and leaned forward. "I'm concerned about Dani."

"If you are worried about me honoring my agreement with her, don't be. I haven't heard back from the private investigator." Jackson ran a finger over the rim of his cup. "When the detective contacts me, I seriously doubt he will have had success in finding Dalton Peppers, unless public records indicate Dalton's deceased. For Dani's sake, that would be best case scenario. She could finally put an end to her futile pursuit of..."

Rose pushed a palm at Jackson as if she was a crosswalk guard. Rose rarely asserted her authority with him, but when she did, he had learned early on to back off.

"What happens to Dani if your investigator doesn't find any trace of Dalton?" Rose said. "What happens to Dani when your Richard Ransom assignment comes to a conclusion, one way or another? In other words, Jackson, what is going to happen to Dani when all of this is said and done?"

Jackson's foot accidentally nudged Yogi, which produced a grumpy sound from his former pet. Jackson had been so preoccupied with nailing Richard Ransom, he had not considered an epilogue to their agreement.

"How can I answer those questions, Rose? In a perfect world, Dani would put everything behind her and get on with her life. But Dani and I didn't grow up in ideal environments. It's damn near impossible to bury what we both experienced." Rose's amber eyes bored into him. "Ultimately, it is Dani's decision. I'm out of the equation."

"Allow me to add a second part to my original statement regarding Dani. I'm concerned about Dani and your history with women."

"Come on, Rose. You know that was the old Jackson. Am I attracted to Dani? Hell yes, I still have twenty-twenty vision. Whether you are aware of it or not, Dani has indicated - under no uncertain terms - she is unapproachable by me or anyone else. I will respect her wishes the same way I will honor my agreement with her." He placed his fingers on Rose's hand. "I want to help Dani, not hurt her. She has been hurt enough."

"I'm going to hold you to that, Jackson. I told Dani she could stay with me for as long as she wants. Do you have a problem with that arrangement?"

Jackson had two reasons for not answering Rose. He wasn't sure how to respond to her question. And his cell phone buzzed. He chose to connect the call.

"Jackson, it's Dani," she said in low voice. "Can you hear me?"

"Barely." Jackson pressed the phone hard to his ear. His right hand formed into a fist. "Are you in trouble? Did Ransom make a move on you? Or discover why you are there?"

"Nothing like that. I'm calling because I have information," she said. "Ransom's plant foreman, Mack, asked me to meet him for a drink after work. He said he wanted to get to know me better professionally. We both know that line had nothing to do with work."

Jackson's teeth were grinding. Dani was correct about Mack's intentions. The only surprise was the line didn't come from Ransom. Either way, it was trouble for Dani.

"Don't go, Dani." He ignored Rose's icy stare. "Please, trust me on this. It's not safe."

"I have a feeling Mack is part of the vandalism gang," Dani said. "He told me he had time for a few drinks before he had to do a job for Ransom. I think they are going to vandalize a J King billboard tonight."

"Dani, listen to me. After a week on the job, you don't know this guy. There's a good chance he is as dirty as Ransom, which means you can't trust him. Maybe they know you're a plant. Nancy is a good looking lady, but not nearly as attractive as you. Why would Ransom hit on her, but not you? Tell Mack you're sorry, but you have to take care of your ailing Aunt Rose. Tell him you will give him a rain check when your aunt is feeling better. Please, do not meet with him."

"I already told Mack I would have a drink with him. It's the only way I can find out what they are up to. I'm holding up my end of our bargain."

"Damn it, Dani! Forget our Ransom agreement. We'll find

another way to get the vandalism information. I'm ordering you not to go. It's too dangerous."

"I'm doing this for both of us, Jackson."

What did "for both of us" mean? Dani's mind was set in quick drying cement; no debate he could offer would talk her out of meeting with Mack.

"Where and when are you meeting Mack?" he asked.

"A sports bar called the Hit and Run Saloon at six o'clock."

"Okay, listen very carefully. This is how *we* are going to play this…"

Rose kept shaking her head while Jackson detailed their plan of action. His gut ached something awful. Not a good sign for Dani or him.

"Promise me you will follow the instructions I gave you," he said.

"Someone is coming, Jackson."

Jackson tried to squeeze the dial tone out of his cell phone.

CHAPTER NINETEEN

Jackson wiped a section of the bar top with a towel. He had frequented enough bars in his drinking days to qualify as a connoisseur. This time he was positioned on the opposite side of the bar after negotiating a quick deal with the manager of the Hit and Run Saloon. One week of free billboard advertising in exchange for Jackson to walk the planks as a bartender for the evening; an expensive but perfect way for Jackson to keep a guardian eye on his corporate spy Dani and the man she was meeting from Double R Outdoor.

Rose sat one table away from Dani, nursing a glass of white wine. Her right hand never strayed far from a purse that concealed a canister of pepper spray. Jackson had not asked Rose to take part in his scheme. She threatened bodily harm if he didn't include her as a member of Dani's protective posse.

Jackson wiped his hands on a towel tucked into the front of his jeans. The room's temperature prompted him to unzip his San Francisco Giants warm up jacket. He left the jacket on in case he had to leave the bar in a hurry.

A drink runner in a low-cut blouse delivered empty glasses from her tray to the bartender next to Jackson and asked for "sex on the beach," presumably the name of a drink and not an offer to romp in the sand. Jackson ignored the shot of Wild Turkey in front of him he pored over an hour ago and thumbed through a bartender drink guide. Passing a law bar exam would be easier than learning the names and ingredients of many of the drink requests. "Sex on the beach" consisted of vodka, peach schnapps, and a combination of cranberry and grapefruit juice - a healthy concoction with a kick.

Dani was wearing designer jeans and a blue turtleneck sweater. She was seated at a small round table next to a man Jackson didn't recognize, presumably Mack. He sat a few inches taller than Dani, had curly dark hair, an oversized nose, and a bulky upper body. His clothes were all black - stocking cap, sweatshirt, and pants; an outfit one would don to blend into the shadows of nightfall when one didn't want to be noticed. Mack carried most of their conversation, both with his mouth and hands. Dani would sneak a peek at Jackson when Mack looked away or raised a glass full of scotch to his lips; doubles compliments of the rookie bartender.

The Tuesday night crowd was large and loud due to an extended happy hour. Four TV's attached to the walls were broadcasting live or taped sports, adding cheers or jeers to the din of the room. Two legitimate bartenders handled the bulk of the orders, which was fine with Jackson. The bald manager, a massive body builder and one time bouncer, had positioned Jackson so he could keep an eye on Dani. From Jackson's vantage point it was impossible to garner their conversation. Nor did Dani's expressions give anything away. All the more reason for Rose to be nearby.

"Screwdriver in a bucket," a young man wearing an Oakland Raider jersey ordered, while waving a hand at Jackson.

Jackson gave him thumbs up. He knew how to make a screwdriver, but what the hell was a bucket? The smiling bar manager handed him a wide glass, answering his question. Was the smile on the manager's face a reaction to Jackson's ineptitude behind the bar or the free billboard advertising? At least now Jackson could add the word bucket to his bartending repertoire. Whatever happened to orders like neat or on the rocks?

Dani reached for her glass of club soda when Mack abducted her hand into his. He leaned forward, his lips flapping well past the speed limit. Jackson held a vodka bottle in one hand and took hold of a paring knife in the other. The same anger spike Jackson felt when he bashed in Pete Long's face with his catcher's mask and pummeled Lieutenant Figg at the Treasure Island Naval Base officer's club.

"Drop the knife, Mr. King." The manager power-gripped Jackson's left wrist. "Remember our deal. You agreed there wouldn't be no trouble." He padded Jackson's jacket. "Good thing you ain't packing. Otherwise I'd throw your butt out of here. Guns and knives ain't part of our arrangement. Now play nice."

Jackson released the knife. The move had been instinctive. Dani carried a pistol in her purse, but he was ready to protect her at all costs. She deftly removed her hand away from Mack and sipped the soda as if nothing had happened. Did he experience a sudden stab of jealousy for the first time in his life?

"My weapon of choice is a twenty dollar bill." Jackson signaled the manager with a head bob and a smile that everything was cool.

Jackson poured a generous amount of vodka over ice cubes into the glass before filling it with orange juice - screwdriver in a bucket. No doubt the manager would watch Jackson like a leaky dam during a heavy rain storm. If their roles had been reversed, Jackson would have reacted the same way. He delivered the screwdriver to the Raider fan, received a ten spot, and was told to keep the change. Jackson rested the bill on the cash register and repositioned himself to view Dani.

Mack drained all the color from his glass, rose to his feet, and lost his balance. His arms spread to right himself. He was obviously feeling the effects from Jackson's heavy-handed pouring. Mack pointed to his wristwatch, then at the front door. Was he asking Dani to go somewhere with him?

Once again, Jackson tensed. Would Dani actually leave with Mack? Rose had a finger on the pepper spray trigger. Dani answered Mack with a smile, but remained seated. Mack opened his palms to plead his case. Dani shook her head. Mack was unaware he was about to be attacked from both sides. Rose was on her feet, ready to launch the stinging spray of pepper into his face. Mack scrunched his shoulders into a thick neck and headed for the door. He looked back at Dani one last time before vanishing into the night.

A raucous round of cheers rocked the bar, although it had nothing to do with Mack leaving. Dani stared at the front door while patrons shouted out their approval and high-fived each other. She grabbed her purse handles, hugged Rose, and made a beeline to Jackson. Her beaming features could have melted the ice machine.

"Thank you for being here, Jackson," Dani said. "Your presence, as well as Rose's, really helped me get through it. I don't know how much longer I could have tolerated that disgusting guy." She shivered like she had walked into a spider's nest. "Mack was unbelievable. He told me I should learn to be a team player. Then he let it slip Ransom gave him first dibs on me as a reward for tonight's assignment. And, get this; if I want to keep my job, I should play along with their arrangement."

"You pulled it off like a pro, Dani, but I'm sorry you had to go through it."

"I'm not sorry," she said. "Your strategy worked perfectly, Jackson. Come on, let's go. I don't want to miss anything."

"Go. Go where?"

"To follow Kenny and your undercover police buddies who are tailing Mack to the billboard they plan to vandalize. We better hurry before they leave without us."

"You did your part," he said. "It took a lot of courage and I couldn't be more proud of you. But you aren't going anywhere except back to Rose's house. It's too dangerous."

Jackson didn't wait for Dani's response. He threw the towel down, scrambled over the bar top, and dodged between tables rushing to the exit door. The night air was invigorating as he ran for his car parked next to the unmarked police sedan and Kenny's truck, except two of the vehicles were gone. On the road fronting the bar, he could see the sedan and the truck taillights disappear from sight. In less than a minute they would be speeding onto the freeway. The sting was in full swing without him.

"Damn it!" He kicked the Mercedes back tire. "I wanted the satisfaction of being a witness to the police taking down Ransom's men."

"You still can." Dani clutched the blonde wig in her hand. "I know which billboard they chose to damage. Only this time they aren't interested in vandalizing the board; they're going to burn it to the ground. I swear, you must have mixed Mack's drinks with Sodium Pentothal."

"Why didn't you tell me this first thing? Which board are they going to torch, Dani? Come on, before it's too late."

"I will tell you once we are in your car and on the way there," she said. "You aren't going to bargain your way out of this one, Jackson."

He pointed to the passenger side door. "Get in."

CHAPTER TWENTY

Jackson punched the gas pedal down sending the speedometer needle a notch under eighty. The Mercedes zoomed past Belmont's Ralston Avenue turnoff heading south on Highway 101 towards San Jose. Dani stretched the limits of her seatbelt by bracing both hands against the dashboard.

The J King billboard Ransom chose to victimize was a one-sided all wood freeway showing in between the peninsula cities of San Carlos and Belmont. Jackson had helped rebuild this structure - illegally - in the dead of night when he first started working for Andrew Lloyd in an era before metal construction became in vogue and there were fewer restrictions. Over forty thousand cars were exposed to the board's ad face daily, factoring out to well over a million impressions per month.

"Richard Ransom knew what he was doing when he chose this billboard to torch," Jackson said. "It was a brilliant yet dastardly move on his part."

"Being an artist, I get the creative part of outdoor," Dani said. "But I've never been privy to the business end. Why is this billboard different than any of your other boards?"

"Since Lady Bird Johnson's beautification act in 1965, certain billboards cannot be rebuilt and/or modified. This board is one of them. If the structure burned to the ground or got badly damaged, I wouldn't be able to replace it. Or the hundreds of thousands of potential advertisement dollars the board would produce. My company would be devalued if and when I decided to sell, favoring Richard Ransom all the more. Eliminating this board would be a win-win for Ransom - he lusts to buy my whole plant of billboards."

Jackson eased off the accelerator and pointed at an illuminated billboard across the highway; the board Ransom had chosen to hit. Dani released the seatbelt and angled her body close to Jackson to get a better look. The advertiser, a car dealership, had been a J King

Outdoor client for years. A painted red banner, referred to as a snipe in billboard talk, had the words "Super Sale" across a corner of the board.

Jackson maneuvered into the slow lane to take the San Carlos Holly Street exit. He turned left at the green stoplight, drove over the freeway overpass to the other side of the highway, and parked on a dirt cutout next to the police undercover vehicle and Kenny's truck. The cutout led to a paved side road that ran parallel to the freeway.

"How did you know to take the San Carlos exit instead of Belmont?" Dani asked.

"Calculated guess." He switched off the engine. "Once you told me where Mack was heading, I knew which billboard they were after. I figured Kenny would also be on the same wavelength. Ransom's men would take the first exit because it's closer. Kenny guided the cops here so they could approach the vandals from the opposite direction."

"Impressive, Sherlock." She opened the passenger door, causing the ceiling light to come to life. "I assume you will provide the same detective instincts when we pursue Dalton."

Jackson turned to face Dani while keeping a hand on the steering wheel. She was so hyper-focused on locating Dalton Peppers, everything else was centered on that priority. Dani's role to play the seductive spy was purely motivated by her need for Jackson to help her. Rose had been right to warn him. What would happen to Dani and her search for resolution if they were unsuccessful in tracking down Dalton? The bullets in her gun would have no affect on Dalton's ghost. Would she continue her fruitless pursuit?

"Wait." Jackson extended his arm out in front of Dani without touching her. As good as she looked in her blonde wig, she was even more attractive as a natural brunette. He had to keep reminding himself Dani was off limits. "I'm not going to try and talk you out of going with me. Hell, you wouldn't listen anyway. Bottom line, it might be safer at the scene of the crime than if I left you out here alone."

"Very chivalrous of you, Jackson."

"I had to give my word to the police I would stay back out of their way. Now you have to promise me you will do the same thing, Dani."

"I promise," she said. "Now, if you would please remove your arm, we might get to see all or part of a real live police drama."

Jackson led the way shining a small flashlight beam three feet on the ground in front of them. Dani enveloped her hands around each arm. She wasn't used to the Bay Area's climate, especially at night. He wrapped his warm up jacket around her shoulders.

"Thank you." Dani snuggled into the jacket and zipped up. "Your coat smells like you - I mean your cologne is nice. I'm sure you are well aware Rose is the President of the Jackson King fan club. She never tires from telling me how good you have been to her. From my standpoint, you are the most generous person I have ever met. And most courteous. Rose confirmed you were once a big time playboy. Good thing she also shared you changed your ways, otherwise I'm not sure if I would feel thankful or insulted."

"If anyone else had said that to me, I'd tell them not to flatter themselves."

"Lighten up, Jackson. I was just joshing. I appreciate your respectfulness more than you will ever know. I guess I'm super-excited about the potential of your plan to take down Richard Ransom coming to fruition." She hitched a purse strap on her shoulder. "But I'm interested in knowing what brought you to your come to Jesus moment?"

"You mean, why did I stop messing around? My psychiatrist explained the reason I needed to behave that way. It goes back to what Dalton did to me, creating a seed of embarrassment and shame I had been trying unconsciously to counteract by proving my masculinity with women."

Dani's shoe found a rut in the road. She stumbled and lost her balance. Jackson caught her by the crook of her elbow before she went to the ground.

"You'd never know I was a country girl from West Virginia, would you?" She disengaged her arm from his hand. "Thank you again, Jackson."

The illuminated car dealership ad came into view. So did a dark object moving towards them on the road. Dani reached inside her purse. Jackson snatched the purse handle away from her before she could remove the gun.

"Hey," Kenny whispered. "Didn't expect to see you both. Saw your lame miniature light, Jackson. Put it back in your purse. It's blackout time on the way back."

"I will remind you of that wisecrack the next time we negotiate a raise." Jackson turned off the flashlight and handed the purse to Dani. "What's happening, Kenny?"

"Two of Ransom's men are waiting at the board for someone or something," Kenny said. "The plainclothes guys want to catch them in the act; a good news, bad news scenario. Catching them after the fact actually means they will set fire to the structure before being arrested. It was a smart idea to bring along fire extinguishers. I hope we can get to the base before the fire gets out of hand."

Kenny led Jackson and Dani to his vantage point, about fifteen yards behind the police who were hiding behind large bushes with their guns drawn. Mack, the smaller of two Ransom men, conversed with his lanky partner under the billboard lights in loud voices to compete with the highway traffic. Kenny passed an extinguisher to Jackson and pointed to which end of the standard he would take if and when the fire started.

Dani crowded next to Jackson, her side against his. He certainly didn't mind the contact, but also realized any physical touching with Dani had to be on her terms. Was it a compliment Dani semi-trusted him?

A light came bouncing towards them from the opposite direction. The taller vandal blinked a signal to the approaching light.

"Ransom is going to be real pissed off," Mack said. "Best be prepared to have a good excuse. I'm not going down with you on this one."

"I hire fucking idiots," the approaching man said in a raised voice. "When one gets an order to set fire to a billboard, what is the first thing one should think to bring? Which one of you dumb shits brought a lighter that doesn't work? Un-fucking-believable."

Jackson and Dani exchanged a look. The voice was familiar to both of them. It came from the bloated figure of Richard Ransom.

"It's my fault, Mr. Ransom." The taller man sparked his lighter several times without getting a flame. "The damn thing was working fine this morning. Since we knew you were close by waiting for us at the Belmont exit restaurant, we thought it'd be easier if—"

"Whatever your name is, you'd be wise to button it." Ransom turned to Mack. "I'm blaming you for hiring this doofus and for not bringing a spare lighter or matches. This is what I get for giving you first dibs at the new cutie artist. I'm taking back that perk for myself." He shined his flashlight on the J King Outdoor insignia, then at the ground in front of the billboard. "I'm surprised you even got the right board to set on fire. At least you collected enough dried brush around the base to make this baby go up in a hurry."

Without switching off his flashlight, Ransom removed a lighter from his coat pocket and with one flick produced a flame. His men followed him to the middle of the billboard base. He bent down, lit the shrubbery, and backed up when a fire quickly started.

"Police!" one undercover cop yelled as they rushed to the gang with their revolvers leading the way. "Stop right there. Hands up where we can see 'em. Do it now!"

Jackson and Kenny sprinted to the base and extinguished the fire before it could spread upward. Kenny continued to spray the area for renegade sparks while Jackson turned and confronted Ransom. One of the undercover guys handcuffed Mack's hands while the other cop held the three at gunpoint.

"We didn't do anything," Mack said. "Richard Ransom was the one who lit the sucker. We were taking orders from our boss."

"Keep your friggin' trap shut. My lawyer will take care of everything." Ransom's head jerked when he recognized Jackson. "King. You son of a bitch. You set me up. How did you know it was me? Did you bribe one of my crew? Bug my office?"

"It was a matter of logic." Jackson held onto the fire extinguisher with both hands. "You're a sleazeball and not one of your billboards was ever vandalized. Getting caught in the act of committing arson is a very serious crime, Ransom. Based on your history, I doubt your sentence will be lessoned for good behavior. This might be the right time for us to negotiate my purchasing your billboard plant since you won't be around to run it."

"You scum sucking dog." Ransom swung the flashlight at Jackson's face. Jackson ducked and shoved the fire extinguisher into Ransom's groin as hard as he could. Ransom went to the ground holding his injured privates and screaming in pain. Jackson stood over him and kicked dirt over Ransom's body the way a dog would bury his crap.

Dani sidled up next to Jackson with a determined look in her eyes. She grabbed the fire extinguisher and sent a direct blast into Ransom's face, making him choke for air.

"I'm nobody's perk, Ransom," Dani said. "By the way, I'm giving you my two second notice. I quit." The extinguisher fell on Ransom's zipper. "Oops!"

Ransom howled as Dani moved away.

"I see why Jackson carries your purse, Dani," Kenny said.

She laughed. "Jackson, Rose said you're a man who gets what he wants. I can see why."

"Not always, Dani. Some things are unattainable."

Jackson's cell phone rang out. A sick feeling made him shudder. He never considered turning off his phone. The whole sting would have been spoiled if this call came a few minutes earlier, warning Ransom's gang before they were caught in the act. Timing in the business world was everything - as well as in the world of crime.

Jackson answered the call, holding a hand over his free ear to block traffic noise. The reception quality was poor; fading in and out.

"Hello, hello. Damn it. His call dropped."

A myriad of emotions pulled at Jackson as he hit numbers to get his caller back.

"What's wrong, Jackson?" Dani said. "Was it bad news? Did someone die?"

"The call was from Whitey, my private investigator. He found Dalton Peppers. Alive."

CHAPTER TWENTY-ONE

L ast night's cell phone call with private investigator George "Whitey" White had stunned Jackson. Dalton Peppers was alive and could be found in a Sacramento hospital. The light at the end of Dani's long quest to find the man who molested her was finally in sight and shining bright. Dani had held up her part of their agreement, now it was Jackson's turn to honor his phase of the deal - even if he had major misgivings.

Dani's mood was upbeat when he picked her up at Rose's house at 6:00 a.m. to avoid Bay Area traffic. She was wearing jeans, a red blouse, and high top moccasins - the same outfit she had on when they first met. The only exception, this morning's makeup highlighted her attractive features. He doubted Dani slept much last night after nailing Ransom. She had to be running on adrenalin; a commodity that could put a fast growing company like Starbucks out of business if it could be ground up and poured into a cup.

Jackson had made good time on I-80 as they headed east away from San Francisco until they sped past Vacaville. He had not counted on a stretch of Sacramento Valley fog. The area surrounding the town of Davis was hidden by a haze of moist air. Dani's demeanor transformed from buoyant to uneasy as they progressed closer to the hospital; an attitude swing likely due to a combination of weather conditions and the proximity of a patient named Dalton Peppers.

"Take the next turnoff, Jackson." Dani studied a Sacramento area map with the overhead light on. "If you remember, we have fog in West Virginia, but nothing like this."

"It's called Tule fog - from late fall to winter." Jackson tilted forward with both hands on the steering wheel, squinting as he veered onto the off-ramp. "Fog-brained drivers who think they can beat these conditions often wind up in a hospital or the morgue."

"Turn right, then take a quick left, I think." Dani's finger was pinned to a spot on the map. "It's difficult to get a gauge where we are when you can't see street signs."

Jackson followed Dani's instructions. He could locate all twenty-nine of his Sacramento area J King billboards in a dense fog without the use of a map, but he was unfamiliar with the location of its hospitals.

"With all of last night's craziness," Dani said, "I never got a chance to ask you what is wrong with Dalton. Why is he in a hospital?"

"Whitey didn't say. His assignment was to find Dalton for us, which he did. Whoa..."

An outline of a tall building appeared through the haze. They passed a sign that may have had the word Hospital. On the other hand, they could be circling an office or apartment complex. Jackson leaned back when a low-lying hospital parking lot sign came into view.

"I tip my pilot's hat to my co-pilot. Nice job navigating us here, Dani." Jackson found a parking space, turned off the engine, and opened the glove compartment in front of Dani. His arm stayed extended without touching her. "Put your gun in here."

"This gun goes everywhere I go." She clutched her purse with both hands. "Before you jump into negotiation mode, giving up my gun is a non-negotiable item. If you don't heed my words, you will have a POW on your hands."

"Prisoner of war?"

"Pissed off woman. Now, please remove your arm."

Jackson placed his hand on the back of Dani's hand firm enough to get her attention, but not to trap her. At one time, he would have helped Dani load her gun. Even now a part of him would love to empty a load of bullets into Dalton. Hate can do that to a person. He loathed what Dalton did to him - even more for what Dalton did to Dani. Yet killing Dalton wouldn't make either one of them whole again. Bringing a lethal weapon to confront their serial molester would only open the door to a number of possibilities - none of them good. Conversely, he also understood why Dani didn't feel secure without her pistol.

"I get why you don't want to relinquish your gun, Dani." Jackson said. "But I want you to consider the whole picture. Bringing a gun into the hospital room of your abuser is a bad idea. Please leave your gun here in the car."

"Are you serious, Jackson? You, of all people, should be elated I came here to confront the blight of our past and create an opportunity for a future. At least it's that way for me, maybe not for you."

"I promised to help you find Dalton," Jackson said. "That part of my agreement is now satisfied. You told me you couldn't bring yourself to kill him. You may have believed it then and maybe even now, but when push becomes pushed-to-the-limit, you have no idea what will happen. Nowhere in our contract did I agree to take part in a murder or someone getting hurt. Leave the gun here, Dani, so there can be a peaceful afterwards."

"Don't you get it?" she said. "There is no afterwards for me if I know Dalton can still get at me or I can't get my frames back."

"I do get it," he said. "I'm all for that sick pervert getting his just due. What if Dalton says something and it sets you off? What if you pull the trigger in a fit of rage and kill a defenseless man? If you run away, they will find you. Don't forget, you found me - we found Dalton. What if you are convicted of first degree murder? In this state they inject you to death instead of being electrocuted by old sparky. Or you will spend the rest of your days in a different kind of prison, one with steel bars or padded walls. Either way, the opportunity to obtain the frames your father gave to you will be gone forever."

"A gun pointed at Dalton could make him tell me what he did with my frames."

"I believe in options, Dani. You have a choice. Put your gun in the glove compartment or I will physically take it away from you."

"Some choice." Dani wriggled her hand free from his grasp, placed her gun in the glove compartment, and kicked the door shut with a knee. She opened the car door and swiveled her body to land both moccasins on the pavement. "Are you coming with me or not?"

Jackson was surprised Dani gave up the gun so easily. He marched stride for stride with Dani through the entrance. No two hospitals looked or smelled alike. They followed wall signs to an information station. Dani's zipped up black purse - minus the security of her gun - still hung heavy on her shoulder. Jackson swiped at a sweaty neck. Although he hated guns, he was having second thoughts about leaving Dani unarmed and feeling vulnerable; yet safe was better than the alternative. They stepped forward as a couple to greet a woman wearing a pink dress over a white blouse. She peered up at him while tucking loose salt and pepper strands of hair back in place.

"How may I help you folks?" the pink clad lady asked.

"My husband and I have traveled a long way to see a patient named Dalton Peppers," Dani said. "Dalton is my brother. Could you please tell us what room he is in?"

"Oh my, that is an easy one," the hospital volunteer said, pushing her printout list to the side. "Your other brother was here a few minutes ago. Mr. Peppers is in an isolated room on the third floor, number 308. Make sure you tell the nurses at their station you are family, otherwise they won't let you in. I told your brother the very same thing."

"Room 308," Dani repeated. "Recently, we were informed about Dalton being here. Can you tell us what is wrong with him?"

"I'm sorry. Even if I had that information, I'm not allowed to give it out." The lady leaned forward. "However, the fact that your brother is in an isolated room on the third floor is all you need to know about his condition. Wish I had better news."

"We haven't seen the brother you saw in years," Jackson said. "He's kind of the black sheep of the family. Can you give us his description so we can recognize him?"

"I don't think you can miss him. He has a beard and long red hair. And he's tall."

Jackson had to take two steps to Dani's one to catch her on the way to the elevator.

"I don't have another brother or stepbrother, Jackson." Dani lips hardly moved. "Nor does Dalton Peppers."

"Dani, you are not the only person who wants to settle a score with Dalton. Let's get security—"

A *ding* sounded. The elevator doors opened. Dani sprinted

ahead to catch the doors before they began their journey to meet in the middle. Jackson ran to catch her. Dani shimmied through the opening before the doors closed.

"Dani, hold the door! Wait!"

The elevator's overhead light glowed by the time Jackson made it to the sealed doors. His fist hammered on the metal as he abused the UP button. He stopped pounding and ran for the entrance leading to the stairs. At the third floor landing, he darted to the nurses' station. Out of breath, he waved both hands in the air to get two nurse's attention.

"My wife passed through here to see her brother Dalton Peppers," Jackson puffed out to the nurse who was standing. "Which way is room 308?"

The sitting nurse pointed at a hallway to her left. "Four doors down on your right. Her other brother is there too."

"We don't even know what's wrong with Dalton. Can you please tell me his condition?"

"Your wife's brother has AIDS." The standing nurse shrugged her shoulders at the other nurse as if she had done something unethical. "Good thing the family came today. Mr. Peppers is getting progressively weaker. I don't think he has much longer."

A booming gunshot rang out from the vicinity of room 308. The nurses exchanged stunned expressions. Jackson slammed his hand down on the counter.

"Call security and the police now." He backed away. "The man with red hair and a beard came here to harm Dalton. Keep staff and patients away from the room until it's safe."

Jackson dashed down the hall. Dani had no way of knowing she could be a victim of prey again. Why did he make her store the gun in his glove compartment? His fingers formed into fists as he readied himself for whatever situation he might find in Dalton's room. He opened the door slowly until he got a full view.

Nothing could have prepared Jackson for the scene before him.

CHAPTER TWENTY-TWO

The presence of gunpowder occupied the air in hospital room 308 as Jackson entered in silence. Dani was lying motionless on the linoleum floor; several feet from a gun. For a nanosecond, he flashed back thirty-five years to his father's wheezing last breath in their West Virginia kitchen. But that scene didn't have a bearded man holding a pillow in both hands standing over a bedridden emaciated looking patient. Jackson didn't recognize Dalton Peppers' gaunt features from the doorway.

Jackson dropped to his knees and scooted in front of Dani to protect her from another attack. There was no sign of blood from a wound. He placed the back of his hand under her nose and sensed puffs of life. Thank God. He gave her soft cheek a reassuring caress, before securing a familiar looking pistol. The gun was a twin to the one left in his car. Damn, she duped him. Dani had carried two guns in her purse. He aimed the short barrel at a tall man who posed his way into the room on the pretense of being Dalton's brother.

"It took me years to track your whereabouts on Highway 80 from Rocklin to Colfax." The man positioned the pillow in front of Dalton's face. "I want what you stole from me and the others. I'll smother you to death if you don't tell me where to find it."

Dalton cranked out a phlegm-filled laugh that brought on a sickening coughing spell. His body spasmed with each hack.

The bearded man inched the pillow away and waited for Dalton to catch his breath. The man's jeans and boots were stained with paint splotches. He wasn't aware Jackson was in the room holding a gun on him. The nightstand's drawer sat on the floor next to Dalton's spilled personal property: shabby wallet, coins, a man's dog tag chain necklace holding a gold colored key, pocket knife, ring with a chipped stone, watch, and keys on a keychain.

"Go ahead and kill me," Dalton finally choked out. "Please, you'd be doing me a favor."

"Drop the pillow onto the floor, Red." Jackson extended the gun at the assassin. His command sounded silly, but a pillow meant to suffocate what little life Dalton had left was as lethal as a gun. "I don't want to shoot you, but I will if I have to."

The would-be killer turned away from Dalton and frowned down at the gun in Jackson's hand with piercing dark eyes. He was younger than Jackson and Dalton - maybe in his early thirties. How did he get the advantage on Dani? Jackson suppressed the urge to take a quick look at her. Most likely, when she entered the room with gun number two in hand the fake brother must have surprised Dani with an overpowering punch - maybe to the head - sending her to the floor. The gun may have fired when her hand hit the linoleum.

Jackson resisted looking for a bullet hole. He was sure of only one thing: the man before him was hell bent on finding the location of the stolen valuables, and determined to prevent any other person from questioning Dalton.

"Who the hell are you?" the man growled, holding the pillow with both hands.

"Someone who is going to stop you from murdering Dalton Peppers," Jackson announced. "The pillow isn't going to shield you from the bullets in this gun."

Jackson had not fired a gun since his hunting days as a child in West Virginia. Was Dalton's assassin daring Jackson to shoot by dis-obeying his command to drop the pillow? Or maybe this guy sensed Jackson's reluctance to pull the trigger. How ironic; Jackson was protecting Dalton with the same gun Dani brought to confront him.

"Afraid to do the dirty deed, Lester?" Dalton's voice was feeble. "The things I stole are in storage. You'll never find where I hid them. You promised to kill me. Do it."

Jackson's head shot back. Lester? Dalton identified this man, calling him by his first or last name. Dalton confirmed he had the items he stole from his victims in storage.

"Dalton sexually molested you as a child, didn't he, Lester?" Jackson said. "Afterward, he took something that held great senti-mental value to you."

"Not only sentimental," Lester spit out. "Dalton took somethin' my granddaddy gave to me in secret. How'd you know what he did to me?"

"You think you're the only person Dalton abused?" Jackson said. "He molested me and many other kids through the years. I understand your desire to kill Dalton. But look at him. If your motive is to hurt Dalton, I mean really hurt him, let the son of a bitch agonize in his last hours from the result of his sick behavior. Can't you see he's lying on death's doorstep, ready to take a fiery plunge? It would be a fitting way for him to go."

"Why'd the woman come in here with a gun? I'll tell you why. To make sure Dalton would tell her where he hid all of our stuff and to kill him so nobody else can have them."

"She carries a weapon for protection as a result of what Dalton did to her as a child."

Dani moved her head and groaned. A good sign, yet she would be better off staying unconscious until hospital security apprehended Lester. What was taking them so long?

"Cut the act, pal." Lester eyed Dani. "We're all after the same thing. You ain't gonna stop me from taking all the treasures this pervert swiped. I've been waitin' a long time for this moment. He ruined my life, now I'm gonna end his and reap the benefits."

"What did Dalton take from you, Lester?" Jackson asked.

"None of your friggin' business."

"Coins," Dalton panted out. "Gold coins."

"You still got 'em, Peppers?" Lester growled. "Or did you cash them out? My granddaddy said I'd be a wealthy man with them coins. I want 'em back."

"That's rich." Dalton went into another coughing fit.

"If you murder Dalton, you'll never recover what he took from you or anyone else."

"Then neither will you." Lester dropped the pillow and reached into his jacket vest pocket, keeping a direct sightline on Jackson. "You don't have the balls to shoot me."

If Lester removed a weapon from his pocket, could Jackson pull the trigger - something he vowed to never do again? The gun in Jackson's hand felt heavier by the second. Time was running out.

Lester had no intention of walking out of this room leaving anyone alive. A vision of his father's last image resurfaced.

"You're in no position to dictate the conditions, Lester," Jackson said in a confident tone. "I'm the one holding the gun. Besides, you don't need Dalton. I know where he hid the duffle bag and I'm willing to share that knowledge with you. But first, you need to take your hand out of your pocket slowly. Very slowly."

"Don't listen to him, Lester." Dalton gasped. "No one knows where I stored the stuff."

Lester inched a hand from his vest pocket hiding something and stepped forward.

Jackson's finger massaged the smooth trigger. He was having trouble swallowing. A rush of air escaped from his mouth when Lester didn't uncover what Jackson was expecting. Instead of a gun or a knife, Lester's fingers were wrapped around a pineapple-shaped, olive green hand grenade. Lester pressed the lever into the grenade's body and pulled out the trigger ring. Holy exploding shit.

"You've got a gun, but I'm holding a grenade which will be activated if you shoot me. We all will die, including the woman. What do you think about your position now?"

Lester had called his bluff with a better hand. Or was it. Jackson couldn't tell if the grenade was real or a fake. If Lester was pulling a con, his team scored a major point since it negated the power of Jackson's gun. How many seconds did Jackson have before the grenade exploded once Lester released the lever? Even if he could get to the bomb in time, then what? Throw the damn thing at the closed window and pray it wouldn't cause even more damage. What would happen to Dani? Jackson's left hand joined his gun hand to stop the shake. How do you negotiate with a demented man holding a grenade?

"I'm your best bet if you want to get your gold coins back, Lester," Jackson said.

"Talk to me, man." Lester's fingers played with the springy lever. "And make it quick."

Jackson could hear ticking. Was it the bomb? Or imaginary? This was one negotiation where everyone would lose if he didn't close the deal.

"I don't give a diddly damn about your coins, Lester," Jackson said. "But we do want to take back what Dalton stole from the lady and from me; they don't hold any value like gold coins. I'll take you to where Dalton stashed the duffle bag if we have a deal."

"No way, assbite. Tell me the location or I'll—"

Dalton screamed in pain after yanking out a tube feeding into his arm. Blood spurted from a vein. He ripped away oxygen prongs from his nose and gasped for air.

Lester fired the grenade overhand at Jackson's head and back-pedaled to the bed. Jackson ducked, threw himself over Dani, and counted. At seven, his eyes opened after there was no detonation. The fake grenade was lying harmlessly against the wall.

Dani stared at him with a dazed expression, blinking several times attempting to focus. Her pupils were dilated. Obviously her brain wasn't firing on all cylinders, but she was alive. Jackson aimed to keep it that way.

Hanging tubes and bags of fluids rocked back and forth when Lester attacked Dalton.

Jackson rolled away from Dani. He aimed the gun at Lester. His finger jumped off the trigger, fearing he might hit Dalton. Leading with the gun, he rushed to the bed and tackled Lester. Dalton cried out in agony from the weight of two men tussling on top of him. Jackson lost hold of the gun as they tumbled off the bed and onto the floor.

On their knees, Lester procured a knife from somewhere, clicked open the blade, and lunged at Jackson. Jackson's forearm defended the smarting jabs. Lester regrouped and came at Jackson with a powerful thrust. Jackson lost his balance. Lester struck again, this time plunging the knife deep into Jackson's thigh. Jackson growled in agony and stared in disbelief at the knife embedded in his leg. A circle of blood formed on his pants.

He stretched to grab hold of the hilt, but Lester got there first and knocked his hand away.

"BOOM!"

The room vibrated. Jackson's ears were ringing. Lester's eyes narrowed in horror at what was left of Dalton's face. The bloody remains splattered against the wall and headboard. Dani's gun dropped to the floor followed by Dalton's body.

Lester stared down at the knife buried in Jackson's thigh, then jumped to his feet. He started for the door, tripped over Jackson in his haste to escape, but managed to stay upright. The door slammed into the wall when Lester threw it open.

"Help, they shot Dalton Peppers," Lester yelled. "They're trying to kill me. Help..."

Jackson rolled his head to the side. Dani was lying still, unconscious. He reached for the knife with his blood soaked arm, but didn't have the strength to pull it from his leg. Loss of blood made him feel faint. He managed to slide his body on the linoleum to one of Dalton's possessions that intrigued him when he first noticed it. His head bounced down on the hard floor after stuffing the item into his pocket. Where the hell was security?

CHAPTER TWENTY-THREE

A broad-shouldered man wearing an unbuttoned, ill-fitting suit jacket that partially exposed a shoulder-holstered gun entered the Emergency Room cubicle as the doctor finished stitching the wounds on Jackson's thigh and arm. His eyes examined the lines of black sutures binding swollen skin that gave Jackson's left side a Frankenstein effect. The doctor nodded to the man while attaching bandages and gauze over the stitches.

"I've often wondered who does the sewing in your house, doc." The man ignored Jackson and removed a small notebook and pen from his shirt pocket.

"My wife, detective." The doctor peeled off his rubber gloves and deposited them on a metal tray next to bandage wrappings. "If she worked in ER, there would probably be a button attached to each stitch." He peered down at Jackson. "You were lucky, Mr. King. It could have been a lot worse - even fatal if the blade had hit a major artery. Pharmacy has your antibiotic and pain prescriptions. Don't do anything strenuous for awhile. I'd hate to see you pop open my handiwork."

"Can you tell me how Mrs. Travers is doing?" Jackson asked the doctor. "Is she awake?"

"She was awake when I last saw her," the doctor said. "The blow to her head caused a concussion, possibly a grade three. We're carefully monitoring her."

The detective waited for the doctor to leave before flipping over the cover of his notebook. Jackson sat up on the table/bed and frowned at his bloody shirt and pants piled on a chair in the corner of the room that were destined for the clothing morgue.

"Mr. King, I'm Detective Hill." He flashed his badge. "Are you feeling well enough to answer some questions?"

"I have no doubt you want some answers from me, detective," Jackson said. "But I have a question for you that has been buzzing around in my head ever since I entered room 308. What the hell took security and the police so long to get there?"

"Security was told to cover all the exits, safeguard the patients on the third floor, and wait for the police. Our turnaround time was less than five minutes, Mr. King."

"In less than five minutes, Dalton Peppers died, Danielle Travers suffered a serious concussion, and I was stabbed several times. I'm told Lester escaped. Wouldn't it have been more prudent to have security immediately handle the situation? Those five minutes felt like five hours."

"I'm not here to debate our procedures with you, Mr. King. The perpetrator escaped by injuring two security guards who were stationed at the stairs. Need I say more?"

"Sorry." Jackson held up his good arm which was now smarting from multiple shots. "Please excuse my venting. I've already told the uniforms what happened." He pinched the front of his gown and pointed to a stack of folded clean hospital staff outfits on the counter. "Speaking of uniforms, would you please hand me a top and a bottom? Anything is better than a hospital gown, even working garb resembling pajamas."

"You are asking me to aid and abet you in stealing, Mr. King."

"Borrow, detective. If you want me to feel well enough to answer your questions, I *bet* you will *aid* me by procuring a set."

The corner of Detective Hill's mouth dropped. He selected a matching green top and pants and handed them to Jackson. Jackson carefully stepped into pants that were too long. His leg and arm had a sense of numbness, but the tight stitches were irritating.

"Fire away, detective," Jackson said. "Is this your way of comparing my story with what Mrs. Travers told you?"

"Mrs. Travers has no memory of what took place in Dalton Peppers' room, Mr. King. Enlighten me why you and Mrs. Travers were in there?"

Jackson snuggled into the green top. If Dani was experiencing memory loss, it could be helpful in several ways. Or was this a ploy by Detective Hill to trip him up.

"Mrs. Travers was Dalton Peppers' stepsister. She wanted

to pay him her last respects and asked me to join her." Jackson gazed down at his new attire. "Are you aware of Dalton Peppers' background?"

"Based on your earlier statement, Mr. King, Peppers was a serial perv who molested both you and Mrs. Travers as kids. Any idea how many children he abused?"

"My guess would be dozens. Lester is the only one I know about besides Mrs. Travers."

"You told the officers who found you Lester had red hair and a beard. Is it possible Lester was in a disguise - wearing a wig and fake beard - when you tangled with him in Peppers' hospital room?"

"His whiskers and hair were as real as real gets, detective. When we were wrestling on Dalton's bed, I pulled on his hair. Or maybe it was his beard."

"Are you saying," Hill said, "Lester came to the hospital to pay-back Dalton for what he did to him as a child?"

"When I opened the door, Mrs. Travers was on the floor out cold and Lester was in front of Dalton's face ready to smother him with a pillow. You make the call, detective."

"Okay, I get this could be a case of retribution on Lester's part." Hill circled something in his notebook. "However, is it a coincidence that you, Mrs. Travers, and this Lester guy would show up at the same time to confront their molester?"

"Coincidence is one thing; a logical sequence of events is another." Jackson rolled up the bottoms of each pant leg to shorten their length. "I hired a private investigator to find Dalton. Last night, George White, the P.I., called to report where we could find Dalton."

"Will your phone records verify your last statement, Mr. King?" The detective worked his pen on a notebook page while he continued to stare at Jackson.

Spikes of anger energized Jackson. Granted, Detective Hill was only doing his job, but the insinuation was insensitive. Maybe he forgot to apply his empathy patch this morning. Or he'd been on the job too long and was jaded. Or maybe he wanted to see how Jackson would react.

"My cell phone records will confirm George White's call last night." Jackson retied the cloth belt. "Have you been involved in molestation cases before, detective?"

"I've had my share."

"Ever wonder how being molested as a child influences a person for the rest of their life? Believe me; it affects all of us differently, but not favorably. And it never goes away."

"Affect a person enough to motivate him or her to murder their abuser?"

"How much money do you make a year, detective?"

"I don't see how that question pertains to this case, Mr. King. I'm sure you're well aware most public servants are on the low end of the salary totem pole."

"I'll give you ten to one odds on your annual salary every person Dalton sexually abused wanted to kill him at some time in their life. Are you a betting man, detective?"

"I get your drift, Mr. King. I also have a feeling, call it detective's instinct, there is something else going on in this case you either don't know or don't want me to know. What is your relationship with Mrs. Travers and why did you hire a private detective to find Dalton Peppers?"

Jackson pulled at his pant leg so the material didn't press against the gauze. There it was; a question the detective had been working up to. Did Detective Hill need to know Dalton stole more than innocence from the people he violated?

"Mrs. Travers tracked me down at my business two weeks ago as a last resort to find Dalton. She was aware Dalton also abused me. We agreed to help each other. She's a very talented artist and I hired her as an independent contractor to deal with a very sensitive business problem. In return, I promised to assist Mrs. Travers in finding Dalton Peppers when her assignment was completed. Although our arrangement is personal in nature, for all intents and purposes, it is a business deal."

"Why the urgency for Mrs. Travers to find Peppers now after all these years?" Hill asked.

"My take on it, detective, Mrs. Travers was searching for a cure. She needed to face the man who instilled a fear that has kept her from living a normal life. That fear was only getting worse. To move forward, she had to confront Dalton head-on for closure. As it turned out, Dalton was dying from AIDS. One look at him should have given her the answer she longed for. I have no idea if she got the opportunity to witness Dalton."

"Well, it almost cost Mrs. Travers her life," Hill said. "What about Lester. Is Lester his first or last name? And what is her history with him?"

"The first time I encountered Lester was when I entered Dalton's room this morning. I don't recall Mrs. Travers ever mentioning a person by the name of Lester."

"The nurses and patients on the third floor heard a gunshot when you were at the nurse's station." The detective pointed his pen at Jackson. "Any idea who fired the gun?"

Jackson stretched his wounded leg. Damn, this guy was persistent. If the detective discovered it was Dani's gun, there would be more questions that would open a whole can of trouble.

"I found the pistol on the floor halfway between Mrs. Travers and the bed. Since there was no sign of blood, I assumed Lester hit her with a fist or the gun, lost his grip, and the gun fired when it hit the floor. Never did see a bullet hole. As I said before, Lester had a pillow in front of Dalton's face. I picked up the gun and threatened Lester to stop or I'd shoot him. All of a sudden, Lester has a grenade in his hand, pulls the ring, and throws it at my head. I hit the deck to shield Mrs. Travers with my body, closed my eyes, and counted out the seconds I had before it exploded."

The detective closed an eye and moved his head side to side as if he was playing the scenario in his mind. If Dani's memory didn't return, they would never know for sure who fired the gun.

"What's your take on the fake hand grenade?" Hill asked. "That is one I have never encountered before."

"Crazy, huh. I thought about it as the doctor was sewing me up. The grenade could have been Lester's fail-safe escape that included taking a hostage. It's the only thing I could come up with. You may have a better version."

"Your take is logical," the detective said. "Who shot Dalton Peppers?"

"You know damn well who shot Dalton," Jackson said. "Dalton started pulling out tubes and needles attached to him. Lester attacked Dalton - maybe Lester wanted the satisfaction of killing Dalton before he did himself in. I didn't want to take a chance of firing a shot and hitting Dalton. So I tackled Lester. I lost the gun on the bed as we wrestled. Dalton found the gun and used it on himself."

"You are saying Dalton committed suicide with Lester's gun without assistance from anyone else?"

"It went down exactly the way I described it," Jackson said.

"What else can you tell me about Lester's appearance besides he had long red hair and a red beard? Height, weight, scars...anything that would help us identify him."

"He's taller than me; maybe he's six-one or six-two. Over two hundred pounds. He's in his thirties. His hands are large enough to hide a grenade. Dark eyes and a fair complexion. His teeth and breath are bad. And he's bowlegged." Jackson made a snapping sound with two fingers. "Lester had different colored spots of paint on his pants and boots, like an artist or a painter. Dalton molested Lester as a kid. Maybe there were other molestation cases in your files or data banks that could be attributed to him."

"As you probably know, Mr. King, most sexual molestations go unreported. But we'll check." Hill flipped to a blank page and kept writing. "What color were the paint splotches on Lester's clothing?"

"Let me think for a second." Jackson closed his eyes. "I never would have thought to ask that question, but it makes sense. The colors were white and a bluish-green...teal."

"Very good, Mr. King." Detective Hill handed Jackson his card. "If there is anything that comes to mind later, please give me a call."

"Sure thing, detective. Now if you don't mind, I'd appreciate a few minutes of private time with Mrs. Travers before you grill the poor woman with questions. She has had a lot of dark moments in her life because of what Dalton Peppers did to her. Maybe I can somehow be a comfort for her."

Walking with a stiff leg, Jackson left the detective. Dani's memory loss was a benefit. However, her memory before entering Dalton's room could get both of them in some serious trouble.

CHAPTER TWENTY-FOUR

Dani was asleep when Jackson limped into her hospital room. Overhead lights were off. On his way to the window he rotated his sore right arm and winced. The pain-killing shots were losing their potency, but he had no complaints about his medical treatment and care. He could also be lying incapacitated in a hospital bed or worse.

The room's only window provided illumination that wouldn't mess with a concussed brain. Dani's doctor offered no timetable for how long the symptoms would stay with her.

A blue-tinted bird flew past the window. Jackson stepped to the sill and peered at the parking lot and moving cars on the surrounding roads. The morning fog was all but a memory. What had transpired in the last twenty-four hours was mind-boggling. With Dani's help, Jackson's scheme to take down Richard Ransom had put his corrupt competitor in jail. Whitey's phone call, however, changed everything. Dalton was dead. Dani was suffering from a serious head contusion and she was fortunate to be alive. To boot, a killer was on the loose. Would Jackson be Lester's next prey?

Jackson turned from the window and studied Dani's comely features as if he was seeing her for the first time. She looked to be at peace with herself and the world. He scooted a chair next to the bed and sat down. He should be furious with her for deceiving him into thinking she went into the hospital without a gun. Instead, he took Dani's hand into his knowing in her current state of unconsciousness she wouldn't object. He was thankful she survived the horror of what transpired in Dalton's room, and annoyed he may never be able to trust her again. If he had confiscated both guns before she entered the room, would Dani be in better or worse condition? A question he'd never be able to answer. Dalton, however, would have died from suffocation rather than his AIDS' virus.

A nurse hustled into the room and stopped at the foot of the bed. After a quick peek at her watch, she jotted something on Dani's chart using a pen dangling from a string necklace. The caregiver had light brown hair and pretty blue eyes above puffy bags. She did a double-take at the man dressed in hospital garb holding her patient's hand.

"You must be *Mr. King*?" She put Dani's chart back. "I thought you'd be bigger."

"I'm Jackson King. Sorry if my size disappoints you. I may have been taller before I entered this hospital. Am I in some sort of trouble?"

"Just the opposite, Mr. King. The rumor mill around the hospital is in full force saying you saved several lives on the third floor." She wiggled her pen. "Maybe I should be asking for your autograph?"

"Unless my signature is on a check, my autograph and a dime has a total value of ten cents. Hate to disappoint you again, but the gossip about me is false."

"My sources tell me different." The nurse gently shook the bed near Dani's pillow. "Mrs. Travers is very pretty. If a man looked at me the way you were looking at her, I'd guarantee him a lifetime of personal healthcare." She shook the bed again. "Due to her head trauma, we want Mrs. Travers to stay awake for the time being so we can observe her. Maybe you can help us to keep her from sleeping for awhile."

"Perhaps we can cut a deal, nurse..."

"Wendy." Her face brightened. "What are you proposing, Mr. King?"

"First and foremost, Wendy, I want you to take care of Mrs. Travers as if she is a member of your family. Secondly, if you dispel the rumor being spread about me, I'll make sure Mrs. Travers stays awake and - here's the kicker - I'll give you an autograph and a dime."

"As an avid coin collector, I'll take that deal."

Wendy jostled the bed harder. Dani's eyelids raised, closed, and settled into half open. Her tongue snaked across dried lips. She swallowed several times and peered at the two people watching her. Wendy lifted a Styrofoam cup filled with water and adjusted a flex-straw to Dani's mouth. Dani panted out breaths after the last sip.

"I'll be back in a few minutes, Mrs. Travers." Wendy set the cup back onto the tray. "In the interim, you have a visitor who has volunteered to look after you while I'm gone."

"Hi," Dani said in weak voice. Her eyes blinked several times. "Why are you holding my hand, Jackson? Am I dying?"

"Based on the doctor's prognosis, Dani, you are going to live a long and healthy life. I'm holding your hand because I didn't want you to wake up thinking you were alone."

"Thank you." Her eyes closed, then opened. "I had the strangest dream. You were with me on a hospital floor - maybe it was Dalton's room. I couldn't talk or move. All of a sudden, you threw your body over mine. It seemed so real."

"I hope you know I would never do anything to harm you."

"It wasn't to hurt me, Jackson. You were protecting me. But I don't know from what. Nor do I recall even going into Dalton's room. All I remember is waking up in ER with a pounding headache and blurry vision that hasn't gone away. What happened?"

Jackson gave her hand a slight squeeze. He didn't want to take advantage of the situation, but he also didn't want to release her hand. Dani's dream had been real. Her eyes opened briefly when he went to the floor in Dalton's room to protect her when Lester threw the grenade. Dani was fortunate she didn't remember. When he had been in the clutches of a Wild Turkey marathon, he would often recall only snippets of the previous evening. If he related what happened in Dalton's room now, it would only make her head hurt more.

"You have a concussion, Dani. Your headache and blurriness should eventually go away. The memory loss, however, maybe not." He squeezed her hand again. "After you woke up in ER, do you remember speaking to a police detective?"

"A man with a crew cut wearing a coat and tie asked me questions. I wasn't much help."

"Did he ask you about your gun?" Jackson's voice hid edginess pulling at his insides. "The other gun you had in your purse?"

"My gun? Oh my God, where's my purse?" She removed her hand from his and placed her fingertips at both of her temples. "What happened to my gun? Did I shoot Dalton? Is that why I can't remember anything? How did I get a concussion?"

"Everything is cool, Dani. You didn't shoot anyone. Nor are you in any trouble. Lets keep it that way. We need to talk about your gun. Why did you deceive me?"

"This is so confusing. I'm sorry, Jackson. You have to believe me, it wasn't to deceive you. I've never been able to go anywhere without a gun. Please tell me what happened?"

"You're right, it is confusing. I'll explain everything when you can better concentrate, but for now you need to trust me." He took her hand again. "Do you trust me?"

"Enough to let you hold my hand while I'm lying helpless in bed." She closed her eyes.

"Open your eyes, Dani." He massaged the back of her hand and waited for her eyelids to creep open. "The police detective, the man in the coat and tie, will be coming to your room soon to ask you more questions. There are a few things he doesn't need to know."

Dani's eyes closed. She desperately wanted to sleep. He gently tugged until her eyes blinked open, then started to close again.

"Stay with me, Dani. Let's concentrate on the gun you brought into Dalton's room and the information the detective needs and doesn't need to know. Come on, Dani, open your eyes..."

CHAPTER TWENTY-FIVE

W ith the aid of Jackson's good arm, Dani ventured outside the hospital after two days of being confined to her room. The doctor prescribed a dose of fresh air for his lethargic and pale patient. Her headache remained, but was nowhere near as intense. Nausea, blurred vision, and dizziness had dissipated. Time, not medicine, would be her fixer-elixir.

Jackson was surprised when Dani took his arm on their slow walk. Although the Emergency Room doctor released Jackson from the hospital after being stitched up from Lester's knife attack, Jackson spent the majority of the last forty-eight hours in Dani's room. If she needed to close her eyes or sleep, he would read or doze in his chair. To a great extent, their conversations were centered on how their lives traveled in different directions. Dani opened up to Jackson, but he was careful not to dig too deep or put pressure on her. Conversely, Dani knew more about him than Marie, his shrink.

A rush of wind smacked their faces when the exit doors slid open. Dani's hospital gown was covered by a borrowed green robe Rose insisted she pack. Jackson was wearing a loose fitting jogging outfit, not that he was fit for any strenuous exercise. It was a struggle for him not to favor his left leg. He led Dani towards an isolated round concrete table encircled with built-in seating and an umbrella. Once she was seated, he placed his sunglasses on the bridge of her nose to eliminate glare. She adjusted the plastic arms on her ears and mouthed a thank you.

"I shouldn't tell you this," she said in a deflated voice. "When I woke up this morning and didn't see you it really bothered me."

"I was speaking to your doctor in the hallway so we wouldn't wake you."

"You know, Jackson, before we met that morning in your office, I don't remember a time in my life when I wasn't alone and lonely. You and Rose took away those feelings. When I opened my eyes this morning and you weren't sitting by my bed, it shook me." She repositioned the sunglasses. "Sounds crazy, huh? Maybe I'm feeling sorry for myself."

"You are probably experiencing melancholy - post-trauma blues - which is another concussion symptom. Hopefully, it won't last much longer."

"Or maybe I was frightened you abandoned me after I tricked you into believing I had only one gun. My only defense is I have lived a lifetime of not being able to trust. I'm sorry. I wouldn't blame you one bit if you did walk out."

"Oh, I'm still annoyed you deceived me. I thought we were partners on the same team."

"Is that what we are, Jackson - partners?"

"I would like to think so."

He pinched the silky material away from his wounded thigh. Should he confess to Dani what his thumping heart was telling him? Or would his admission frighten her away?

"The detective told me Lester threw a grenade at you," she said. "Thank God it wasn't real. Was I dreaming or did you throw yourself over me as a shield before it exploded?"

"It doesn't really matter, Dani. The bomb was a fake."

"Now it's you who is trying to mislead me." Her voice was firm. "Yes or no, Jackson?"

"It was a reaction, Dani."

"The blast would have killed you if the grenade had been real." Her blue eyes studied him. "Why would you protect me, especially after I deceived you?"

"I responded without thinking. Leave it at that."

"How about answering a few related questions, like when do you get your stitches out?"

"The doc said in a couple of weeks. I'm on a roll. What's your next question?"

"How did you get the scar on your cheek?"

Jackson's eyebrow jutted into his forehead. A question from left field? He rubbed a fingertip over the scar. How long had she been itching to ask him that question?

"It's probably not from what you are thinking," he said. "Does the scar bother you?"

"No, not a bit." She reached to touch his face, but her fingertips stopped a millimeter away. "By all accounts, you are a wealthy man, so the cost of plastic surgery wouldn't be an issue. Nor has it hindered you from being successful. So, how did you get the scar?"

"I was involved in a car accident late one night driving home from work. Before you ask, I was sober. But the woman who hit me head-on was blotto out of her mind, three times the legal limit. On the way to the hospital in the ambulance it dawned on me; that woman very well could have been me. I can't calculate how many times I drove under the influence. The reality of the accident really bit hard; enough for me to seek help. I haven't had a drink since." Jackson stroked his cheek again. "Another reason I didn't do anything cosmetically; nothing is going to help this mug."

"Nice try, Jackson. Save the false modesty for all the ladies who give you second and third looks. I imagine some women even find your scar sexy."

He cocked his head slightly. Did her last comment include herself? Or was Dani indicating she was the exception?

"There's another reason I don't get it fixed," he said in a serious tone. "The scar is a reminder to never have another drink."

"Now I'm really puzzled. When I was sitting with that slug Mack at the Hit and Run Saloon last week, I noticed a shot glass filled with a whiskey-colored drink on the bar while you were pretending to be a bartender. Was that your drink?"

"Not only was it my drink, it was my drink of choice. Hope you also noted the glass went untouched. Occasionally I challenge my demon to show him I'm stronger than he is."

"You are a fascinating man, Jackson King. Maybe even captivating."

"*Thank you.* Now it's my turn. There is something I've been meaning to ask you. How did you convince Mr. Ornstein in Reno to tell you where I could be found?"

"Mr. Ornstein is so proud of you, Jackson. And protective. He grilled me with questions until I convinced him it was imperative I locate you." A blush came to her cheeks. "But not before he shared a story about your high school sexual exploits and winning over a judge in court. I was very impressed, at least about the courtroom part."

"I got lucky the right presiding judge was at the hearing."

"According to Mr. Ornstein, the judge still sings your praises about how you handled yourself in his courtroom as a teenager."

"Dani! Jackson!" Nurse Wendy hurried to them with her pen on a string swinging. "I'm so glad I caught both of you. I'm on my break. I know you must be tired of me by now, and this sounds ridiculous, but I'm sorry to see you go."

Dani twisted around. Wendy bent forward with open arms and gave Dani a long hug. Jackson grinned. Nurse Wendy was the best medicine any patient could receive, especially a patient like Dani. Whatever wage Wendy earned, it wasn't near enough.

"How could anyone get tired of you, Wendy?" Jackson said. "We are thankful for your excellent care."

"Don't you go sweet talking me, Mr. King," Wendy said, pointing a finger at him. "Have you forgotten the deal we made?"

"To set the record straight, nurse, I did not forget. And Dani will tell you I honor all the deals I make." Jackson removed a business card from his jacket pocket and handed it to Wendy. "I believe this will fulfill my part of our agreement."

Wendy's smile broadened when she flipped the card over and saw a 1925 Liberty Mercury dime taped on the back along with his signature - the same lucky dime Jackson had carried in his pocket for years. She shook her head and pushed the card back to him after scrutinizing the coin again.

"Jackson, do you have any idea how valuable this dime is? I can't take—"

"We made a deal, Wendy," Jackson said, collapsing her fingers over the card. "I hope you aren't the type of person who would renege on a verbal contract. I'd hate to have my attorney get involved in our agreement."

"Your generosity overwhelms me, Jackson. Thank you." Wendy placed the card over her heart before tucking it into her pocket.

"What an awesome couple the two of you make. I'll never forget either one of you."

"It's none of my business," Dani said, after Wendy re-entered the hospital, "but what was the deal you made with her?"

"Do I sense a sliver of jealousy, Mrs. Travers?" Jackson straightened his back. "You should know by now I never deal and tell."

"Not once have I ever been accused of being jealous, Mr. King. Get over yourself." Dani gave Jackson's good arm a light pinch. "For your information, I'm concerned about Wendy. I believe she has a crush on you. For some inane reason Wendy thinks you are rock star royalty that has nothing to do with the last name of King. Now fess up."

"Nurse Wendy made me promise to treat you like a princess until your headache went away. Enjoy it while it lasts, princess. Besides, I'm sure you set her straight about me."

"Why would I spoil Wendy's day?" Dani folded her hands on the table. "Conversely, you keep making my days. I can't thank you enough for your patience and care, Jackson."

Dani looked away and peered at the hospital's snack stand. She turned to him biting down on her lower lip as her features tightened into a somber expression. Lately, the buoyancy of her mood could change as quickly as mid-western weather.

"Some things don't add up," she said. "Why would Dalton commit suicide? Did he all of a sudden get a conscience? And how did he get a hold of my gun to do it? I can't help but think you are protecting me from something. Please tell me the truth, Jackson. Did I kill Dalton? Are you are shielding what really happened from Detective Hill?"

"I'm all for protecting you, Dani, but you did not shoot Dalton. Lester was in the room when I got there. You were unconscious on the floor. Lester was intent on finding the whereabouts of the valuables Dalton stole from all of his victims and killing Dalton. I picked up your gun and tackled Lester on the bed instead of shooting him. In doing so, I lost hold of the gun. Dalton found the gun and shot himself. Lester fled the room. The ironic part; Dalton's last act may have saved both of our lives."

Dani's fingers covered her lips as if she was playing the scene in her head. Jackson could only imagine the multitude of emotions tugging at her. She lowered her hands, but stared straight ahead while breathing hard through her mouth.

"I have hated Dalton Peppers my whole life," she said. "I can't turn a switch and make the hate dissipate. Am I grateful Dalton may have saved your life? You bet I am, Jackson." She sucked in a deep breath. "I never thought I'd say this, but I even feel a smidgeon of sympathy for Dalton, but nowhere near as sorry as I feel for all the people he abused. Isn't it amazing how one bad seed can injure the lives of so many?"

"Great point." He removed his sunglasses she was wearing. "There's also another way of looking at it, though. Close your eyes."

Her back stiffened. A conditioned response he'd come to expect. Her eyelids tumbled.

"Now open your eyes and tell me what you see?"

"Nothing is different," she said, squinting. "What am I missing?"

"There is a difference—a big difference." He placed the sunglasses back onto her nose.

"Never again will you have to fear the presence of Dalton Peppers. The only person who can stop you now from moving forward with your life is you, Dani."

Dani rubbed her arms. Would she ever be able to visualize a world where she was safe? Or unafraid?

"How was it possible for Lester to escape?" she asked.

A question Jackson had hoped Dani wouldn't pursue. He didn't want her to transfer the fear she felt with Dalton to a dangerous, roaming free ogre like Lester. To complicate matters even more, Jackson misled Lester about knowing where Dalton hid the valuables he stole. Lester was now privy to Jackson's name from several newspaper articles. If the police didn't nab Lester soon, chances were he would be coming after Jackson.

"The detective blamed hospital security for Lester getting away," Jackson said. "Don't worry, if the police haven't yet corralled Lester, he's probably in Canada or Mexico."

"Jackson, I never felt right about lying to the detective. If I didn't shoot Dalton, why didn't you want me to admit it was my gun?"

"Put yourself in the investigator's loafers. Why would a woman bring a gun into a hospital room occupied by the man who molested her?"

"To shoot the man who molested her." Dani lifted the robe's collar. "I get the reason, but I'm still not comfortable with it."

"You wouldn't like the alternative either. The detective most likely would have no choice but to arrest you for attempted murder even if you didn't pull the trigger."

"Something I didn't consider." She waited until a lady in a wheelchair rolled by. "Will you explain why you didn't want the police to know about the prized possessions Dalton took from all of us?"

First and foremost," Jackson said, "to the police the valuables Dalton stole are his until proven differently. They aren't going to allow us take our possessions without an investigation. Nor would the police have reason to make the items a priority. If the police recovered the valuables, would they take the time to find and return the items to the victims, one of your goals? Probably not. If Detective Hill was privy to what Dalton stole, he might stop us from doing our search since it could obstruct his investigation. As much as I want my baseball card collection back, finding the frames your father gave to you and helping the other victims is most paramount to me."

"God, what a mess I've made of everything." Dani rubbed her forehead. "You were badly hurt. Security guards were injured. Dalton died without telling us if he had our stuff. And Lester escaped.

Dani cupped a hand over the sunglasses to deflect sunlight the umbrella didn't shield. Tears leaked from underneath the glasses. Jackson stood and tilted the umbrella until it blocked the sun from her face. He gently put both hands on her shoulders and peered at his reflection in the dark lenses. She didn't pull away.

"I thought you would be euphoric after learning Dalton was dead," he said.

"I was so emotionally invested in the idea of ridding my life from Dalton's influence, nothing else mattered," she choked out. "You warned me in the car in the hospital parking lot, but I wouldn't listen. I never considered the collateral damage of my actions. It was all selfishly about me."

"Dalton would have died, either from Lester or from AIDS, whether you were involved or not. Rather than beat yourself up, you should be proud of what you accomplished."

"If you are trying to make me feel better—"

"I'm trying to open your eyes to the real picture," Jackson said. "You now know Dalton will never terrorize anyone again. You are fast becoming the daughter Rose has yearned for. It has been a long time since I've seen her so happy. You were invaluable in solving my problem with Richard Ransom. And, because of your mission, we now know Dalton stashed the duffle bag somewhere in this area."

"How do you know that, Jackson? Even if your wild assumption is correct, a lot of good it will do us. There's no way we can find out where he hid everything."

"Dalton told Lester the valuables were in *storage.*" Jackson dangled a dog tag chain holding a gold key. "Among Dalton's possessions in the room, he had a key ring as well as this key on a neck chain. Quite possibly it is the same key he wore on a chain when he was traveling with my family. Why would this key be more important than the keys on the key ring? Because this key opens a padlock guarding the duffle bag. One key, one location."

"Even if you are right, that one location can be anywhere," she said.

"Where does one store things they consider valuable, Dani?"

"In an attic. Maybe a safe. A locker, garage, public storage…"

"Bingo." He swung the gold key as if he was hypnotizing her. "Lester said Dalton kept moving, starting from the city of Rocklin all the way up Highway 80 to the town of Colfax. To me, it's logical this key will open a lock to a public storage unit between Rocklin and Colfax."

"Oh my god, Jackson. Do you really think we can find the duffle bag?"

"After your doctor gives you a clean bill of health, *partner*, we are going to find the lock that fits this key."

"This is like a treasure hunt." She seized his hand. "Where do we even begin our search?"

"By going to one of my favorite places."

CHAPTER TWENTY-SIX

The nearest public library to the Sacramento hotel suite Jackson and Dani were staying in was undersized compared to San Francisco libraries. So was the parking lot. Jackson pulled his car into one of the two remaining side-by-side vacant spaces.

"If you gave me a hundred guesses, I wouldn't have figured a public library was one of your favorite places," Dani said.

"I don't know why you are so surprised. We've been living together at the hospital and our hotel suite for almost a week now. I would have thought you knew practically everything about me."

"I'm learning more and more each day," she said with a smile. "For example, after you wake up in the early morning hours, you eat a banana before your first cup of coffee. Furthermore, from my bedroom I could hear you sing oldies in the shower - loud and off key I may add."

Jackson raised a hand in surrender. He couldn't carry a tune even if it had handles. Dani's banter was a positive sign she was over her melancholy. Her pupils were back to normal, color had returned to her cheeks, and most of her headaches were a pain in the past. The doctor's biggest concern was for Dani not to take another blow to the head.

"Are you sure you feel up to tackling this project?" He studied her eyes, something he never tired of. "Maybe we should have waited a bit longer to begin our research."

"I'm fine, really. As nice as our suite is, it's great to finally get out. Between living with you and talking to Rose on the phone everyday, I could get a concussion from all of the TLC. Really, I'm not complaining. I guess I caught a case of cabin fever." She unbuckled her seatbelt. "Why are we here?"

"To get listings of all the public storage facilities from Rocklin to Colfax. Libraries carry neighboring town phonebooks."

"How do you know this library carries phonebooks?"

"Years ago when I first started selling ad space on billboards, the yellow pages proved to be a great sales tool for targeting potential clients. I was spending more time in phone booths than Superman. Because I had worked in a library in Reno, I remembered they had several shelves dedicated for phonebooks. Libraries became my phone booth." Jackson removed Dalton's key still on the chain. "Libraries also have copy machines available to the public. We can copy all the city storage facility pages in a few minutes, and then we are off to find the lock that fits this key."

"You have come up with a clever plan." Dani opened her door. "Wait, Jackson. What about Lester? If you figured out how Dalton stored the duffle bag, couldn't Lester have done the same thing?"

"Doubtful. Lester doesn't know about the key." Jackson shrugged his shoulders. Dani didn't need to know he was concerned Lester would come after him.

The age demographic inside the library ranged from junior to senior, placing Jackson and Dani somewhere in the middle. They sat next to each other at a corner table in front of stacks of phonebooks organized by Highway 80 cities, starting with Rocklin and ending at Colfax: Jackson's Plan B. The librarians were waiting for a technician to repair the public copy machine.

Jackson lowered the pile by removing the top phonebook, placing it next to his paper pad and pen, and flipping through the thin pages until he got to the Public Storage heading. Dani mimicked Jackson, only she chose to write the information in pencil.

A girl's giggle made Jackson glance to his right at the children's section. A mother was reading a Dr. Seuss book of rhyme and drawings to her young daughter. Long ago, Dr. Seuss had been one of his favorites.

To the left of the children's section, Jackson's eyes zeroed in on a bald man wearing a faded green t-shirt and holding a *Field & Stream* magazine covering the lower portion of his face. The guy had protruding ears and a pale complexion. He reminded Jackson of an unattractive Mr. Clean - the TV commercial cleaning product character.

Jackson peeked at Dani's pad while she worked her pencil. She had nice handwriting. Plus she was a gifted artist...

"Would you be able to draw a facial composite like a police artist?" Jackson whispered.

"Nowhere near as well as a portrait artist, but I could craft a reasonable likeness if you can articulate what his or her features look like." She pointed the eraser end of her pencil at him. "Why?"

"I should have thought about this before," he said. "Picture a man in his early thirties, longish hair an inch or two below his ears, bushy beard that covered his neck, thick eyebrows, dark serious eyes, thin face, and a longish, narrow nose."

Dani first peered up at the ceiling. On a separate sheet of paper she began a sketch based on Jackson's description. He was in awe watching her create a man's face she had never seen or had no memory of seeing.

"I wish I had your talent." He studied Dani's rough drawing. "The face is close, but something is off. I think he had bangs covering his forehead. A longer nose. Maybe thin the cheeks."

Dani edited the drawing and slid it in front of Jackson. The rendition made his heart rev into a faster beat. It was a rough image of Lester's face, but the sketch mirrored another face. He snatched Dani's pencil and attacked the beard and hair with the eraser.

"What are you doing?" Dani voice drew looks from other tables. "I realize I'm not the greatest portrait artist, but you didn't have to take an eraser to it."

"I'm updating the information I gave you."

Jackson rubbed away eraser remains. The drawing didn't depict Lester anymore. Instead it resembled the man reading the *Field & Stream* magazine, except for the eyebrows. Jackson sent the eraser in motion again.

"Unlike Mr. Clean, the son of a bitch shaved off his eyebrows," Jackson said in a low voice. "No wonder I didn't catch it."

"I have no idea what you are talking about, Jackson."

To confirm his suspicions, Jackson looked under Lester's table. His jeans had splotches of paint. Bald and without a whisker of a beard, Lester's face had changed dramatically. Take away a set of eyebrows and Lester appeared to be a different person. A hair-lift was almost as good as a facelift when one was hiding from the law.

Lester turned the magazine page. Jackson looked down at the drawing. How the hell did Lester find them? Dani's pencil snapped in Jackson's hand. Lester must have followed them from the hospital to the hotel. Jackson's false admission informed Lester he had knowledge where Dalton hid the valuables he stole. Lester was lying in wait for Jackson to lead him to the duffle bag. Time was now an issue. Jackson reached across Dani and snatched the phonebook she was using and ripped out a page.

"Now I know you've flipped out, Jackson. These pages are for everyone, not just us."

Jackson placed a forefinger on her lips. He leaned close to Dani's ear as if he was serenading her with romantic nothings. She didn't back away.

"Our plans have changed," he whispered. "We need to find the public storage info as quickly as possible." Jackson handed Dani a business card from his pocket. "Put this card into your purse. The business card has Detective Hill's cell phone number on the back. Call the detective on your cell phone and tell him Lester is at the library, but he changed his appearance; bald, no red hair or beard, and he also shaved off his eyebrows. Finally, I want you to give me a peck on the cheek before you casually walk to the ladies room to make the call."

"Lester is here?" Her eyes widened. "Oh my God, where is he? Now I know why you've been acting so crazy. And had me do the drawing. What are we going to do if—"

"Don't look for him," Jackson said. "I'm sorry, Dani. In my attempt to keep you safe, I've put you in jeopardy again. Everything will be fine if Lester doesn't know we are on to him. If you can't reach Detective Hill, leave a message and call the police department number on the card's front. Next, saunter back to the table as if nothing is wrong."

"What are you going to do while I'm in the ladies room?" she asked.

"I'll be the decoy." Jackson silently ripped out another page. "If I remain seated Lester won't get suspicious. All we are doing is buying time for the police to show up."

"What if Lester decides to leave before the police get here? Or he tries to kill you again? Jackson, you are in no condition to chase Lester or fight him. I'm staying here."

"Lester doesn't have a reason to suspect we recognized him as long as we don't do anything to raise his suspicion. The key is to get the police here as quickly as possible and for us to act normal."

Dani blew out a frustrated breath, stuffed the card into her purse, and stood. She took a step away, turned around, and planted a soft kiss on his cheek.

"Why did you ask me to kiss you?" she whispered in his ear.

"I want Lester to think we are a lovey-dovey couple enjoying each other, even in a library." Jackson smiled. "And I was curious if you would actually do it."

"Well, now you know." She headed to the ladies room with her purse swinging.

Jackson built a wall of phonebooks in front of him, leaving an inch gap in the middle of two stacks. The magazine remained in front of Lester's face, but his head was twisted towards Dani. Jackson began tearing out pages; pages he didn't want Lester to get his hands on. All hell could break loose before or after the police arrived.

After removing most of the storage pages, Jackson stole a peek at Lester sitting in the same position, almost as if he was staged. Jackson shifted his view to the ladies room door. Hopefully, Dani had reached Detective Hill and the police were on their way.

Jackson slid the last phonebook, Colfax, next to the paper pad and fanned the pages to public storage. A movement to his left caught his eye as he ripped out the page. A female librarian was speeding towards him with a determined look on her face. His stomach quivered the same way it did when he was ten years old and a librarian caught him tearing out a Mickey Mantle article from *Sport Magazine*. He hid the loose yellow page under Dani's pad of paper. Although he was no longer ten years old, he sure felt like it.

"Sir," the librarian said, straightening her glasses. "You are monopolizing a good share of our phonebooks. We would appreciate when you are finished with a book to please replace it back on the shelf and in alphabetical order for others to use."

"My apologies," Jackson said. "I will put them back in the correct order."

"I sincerely hope you aren't ripping out pages," she said, crossing her arms.

"In full disclosure, as a boy I tore out a library magazine article. But I'm an adult now."

"Adults are our worst offenders."

Jackson lifted the stack of phonebooks and took a quick glance at Lester. The books fell from his hands, crashing down on the table. Lester was nowhere in sight.

"Ho shit." Jackson dashed to the bathrooms. The librarian yelled at him from behind. He blasted open the ladies room door. A woman with a walker by her side was washing her hands at the sink. She peered at Jackson's image in the mirror and turned off the faucet.

"Wrong room, bub." She shook her wet hands over the sink.

"Did you see a pretty brunette lady wearing a white sweater, jeans, and moccasins?"

"Nope." She snatched a paper towel. "Maybe you should try the men's room."

Jackson raced out of the library, down the cement steps, and into the parking lot. There were no signs of Dani or Lester. Distant sirens sounded in the background. Was Dani able to contact Detective Hill? Or were the sirens signaling another emergency situation?

He gasped for air. Dani and Lester had disappeared as if they were vaporized. Jackson didn't have to use his fingers to do the math. One plus one equaled Lester had Dani.

CHAPTER TWENTY-SEVEN

Jackson pivoted in circles, shouting Dani's name from the library parking lot. A stiff breeze carrying a hint of moist air made his long sleeve shirt and khaki pants flap like a flag. One second he was spying on Lester, the next moment Dani and Lester vanished as if they were participants in a magic act. But their disappearance was no illusion.

A pale blue station wagon pulled into the lane Jackson was blocking and beeped for him to move. He stepped aside to accommodate the car while hollering Dani's name. The female driver shook her head as if he was unhinged when she motored past him and parked in the only empty space in the small parking lot.

"Yeah, I'm crazy, lady. Crazy with fear."

Background sirens sang louder. Jackson's stomach produced a distress signal of its own. His eyes continued to search for a clue that would lead to Dani's whereabouts. Why would she leave the safe confines of the library? It was inconceivable Lester would nab Dani from inside the building and drag her outside without making a sound or a scene.

Jackson kept turning without knowing what he was looking for. He could think of only one reason Lester would kidnap Dani; to get to the man who falsely claimed he had knowledge of where Dalton hid his duffle bag.

Station wagon lady walked past Jackson with her nose tilted upward. Was it possible she parked in the space Lester vacated after leaving the library? Jackson closed his eyes and tried to visualize the make and model of the vehicle parked in that space when they arrived, but nothing came to mind. His view shifted to his car. He had given Dani a spare key. Maybe she was hiding inside the Mercedes until the police arrived. He recalled seeing only two empty spaces side-by-side in the parking lot when they pulled in earlier. A grey van had backed into the space next to his car.

Jackson ran to the Mercedes. His shoulders slumped after peering through the side windows. He turned to face the library front. Was it possible they were still inside? He had only asked the woman in the ladies room if she had seen a female with Dani's description.

The cell phone buried in Jackson's pocket rang. His first inclination was to ignore it, but an ass-clinching stab of reality made him change his mind. He connected the call.

"I've got your woman, King. You will never see her alive unless you give me the key."

Jackson's ears picked up sirens nearing the library and through his phone. Lester and Dani were close by. How close? If Lester followed them from the hotel to the library, the only space he could have parked in was occupied by the van next to the Mercedes. Lester must have forced Dani to tell him about the key. Jackson resisted an urge to turn around.

"I will give you Dalton's key, Lester." Jackson's pulse was racing out of control. "But not before I know she is alive and unharmed. Let me speak to the lady. "

"She's tied up and has tape over her mouth. You'll have to take my word for it."

"That's not acceptable, Lester. Time's running out. The police are on their way. Unless I talk to her, we have no deal. Look, I've already said you can have Dalton's key. Without me, you will never find your gold coins. I'm offering the key and me for the lady."

"Shit," Lester grunted out. "I need to see the key. One false move on your part and she dies. The knife I left in your leg should tell you I mean what I say. Turn around, King."

Lester posed in the van's driver's seat motioning a knife. Jackson reached into his pocket and dangled the chain and key. Lester twisted around and disappeared into the van's windowless body. A ripping sound was followed by a sharp cry.

"Jackson, he's got me tied up in a van next to your car. He has a knife. I'm so sorry—"

Jackson couldn't understand the rest of Dani's muffled message. Lester must have put a hand or tape over her mouth. She sounded out of breath, frightened, but not in pain.

Jackson's fingers closed over the key to make a fist. What were his options, if any? The sirens were louder, but not loud enough. He could no longer count on the police. Lester was armed and using Dani as leverage. Did Jackson have enough time to retrieve Dani's gun from his car? Would the weapon help rescue Dani or put her in more jeopardy? He opened the driver's side door to his car and removed Dani's pistol from the glove compartment. The gun was a leverage equalizer.

"You win, Lester," Jackson voiced into the phone. He placed the pistol in his back pocket. "Open the side door. Let me see her."

Silence. Dead silence, except for Jackson's heartbeat. He reached for the gun when the van's door slid open. Lester had a knee planted on the metal floor holding his knife in front of Dani. She was sitting up with her ankles and wrists tied with tape.

"Hand me the key and step away," Lester demanded, holding out his other hand.

"Dani, I know you can't talk with the tape over your mouth. Nod if you're okay."

Lester pinned the knife to Dani's sweater. Her eyes bulged as she nodded. The key in Jackson's left palm was cutting into his skin. His right hand inched for the gun.

"Give me the key now, King," Lester snarled. "Or I'll cut her."

Dani's head shook vehemently. Jackson ignored her warning and moved towards the van. Five feet away from Lester's outstretched hand, he let the key drop to the cement. The hairless features on Lester's face scrunched into a fierce expression. The knife blade shifted away from Dani to point at Jackson - exactly what he wanted Lester to do.

Jackson pulled the gun from his pocket as Lester rocketed at him from the van. The gun slipped from his grasp. They fell to the cement with Lester on top of him. Jackson grabbed the wrist of Lester's knife hand before Lester could stab him.

Behind Jackson, a vehicle screeched to a halt at the library front. The police? If so, they arrived without using the siren. If not, Jackson and Dani were in some deep trouble.

Lester maniacally tried to maneuver the knife blade towards Jackson's chest and reach for the key with his other hand. Jackson had both hands on Lester's arm. Lester's head shot up, giving Jackson an opening to gain control of Lester's wrist. Jackson wouldn't let go when Lester tried to rise. Lester punched Jackson's chin, jumped to his feet, and ran from the parking lot into a neighborhood of houses.

Jackson pocketed the key and staggered to his feet. He heard shouts and footfalls behind him as he moved to the van. Dani had rolled towards the opening. He ripped the tape from her ankles, wrists, and mouth and helped her to the cement. She wrapped her arms around him. Her hug produced as much joy as it did pain.

Light rain was falling by the time Detective Hill and two uniforms hit the scene. The detective barked orders to the officers and pointed in the direction where Lester fled the parking lot. He went to a knee to examine the gun.

"Interesting." Hill rose to his feet. "The same gun we found in Peppers' hospital room."

"What a coincidence," Jackson said, without looking at the detective. "You know, I'm beginning to see how happenstance can occur a lot in your business. By the way, your timing was much better than at the hospital."

"Lester said he'd kill both of us unless you gave him—"

"Did he hurt you?" Jackson placed a hand at the back of Dani's head. "Are you okay?"

"I am now," she said. "When I saw Lester leap on you from the van I thought I'd lost—"

"You're sure you are okay?"

"Yes, Jackson. Why do you keep asking me?"

"Because you're hugging me."

"What did you negotiate with Lester to save my life?"

Damn. Detective Hill's keen eyes were zeroed in on Jackson.

"Later," he whispered in her ear.

Detective Hill cleared his throat. "I find the display of affection by two people who have strictly a business arrangement puzzling. There is more to this story than both of you are telling me, starting with why people keep trying to kill you? Why were you, Mrs. Travers, and Lester at the library? Why would Lester abduct Mrs. Travers. Damn it, are you listening to me?"

"It was my fault, detective," Dani said, still holding Jackson. "After I called you from the ladies' room, I inched open the door and saw Lester heading for the exit. I followed him hoping to find the make of his car and to get his license number. When I got outside, he put a hand over my mouth and pulled a knife on me. He baited me into following him."

"Why would Lester have reason to abduct you, Mrs. Travers?" the detective asked.

"Don't get your investigative instincts in a bunch," Jackson said. "My guess is Lester's goal was to kill Dalton for sexually molesting him. But he never got the opportunity because of my interference at the hospital. So he took Mrs. Travers to get back at me. The newspapers depicted me as a wealthy owner of a company. Most likely Lester thought we were a couple. Maybe he was looking for ransom money."

"Is that your take, Mrs. Travers? Or is there another reason Lester seized you?"

She pulled away from Jackson, moved her sticky red fingers together, and gasped.

"Jackson, you're bleeding. Did that bastard Lester stab you again?"

Jackson examined his pants leg and sleeve. "It's probably a busted stitch. No big deal."

"Well it's a big deal to me," she said. "You wouldn't be bleeding like that if—"

"You didn't answer my question, Mrs. Travers. Do you agree with what Mr. King—"

"With all due respect, detective, if you want my cooperation, call an ambulance ASAP for Mr. King. When the ER doctor tells me he is all right, I will answer your questions."

"I don't need an ambulance, Dani."

"Is she always this demanding, Mr. King?" Hill said, raising a radio to his lips.

"You ought to see her when she's *really* on a mission."

"You two deserve each other." The detective pressed a button on his radio. "I need an ambulance at public library..."

* * * * *

The ER cubical remained crowded after the nurse left to assist with another emergency.

Jackson was lying face up with his leg and arm wounds exposed. He couldn't tell who was the most annoyed with him: the doctor, Detective Hill, or Dani.

"Doctor," Dani said, "because you have firsthand knowledge of Jackson's current medical history, maybe you should use double-stitches this time."

"Not a bad idea, Mrs. Travers." The doctor re-sutured broken stitches in Jackson's leg. "You sound much better than the last time you were here. As for you, Mr. King, what did you not understand when you were told not to do anything strenuous for a while?"

"As it turns out, I'm not a very good patient." Jackson shot a quick look at Detective Hill.

"Nor are you a good witness." The detective flipped open his notebook. "I've taken your statements, but I don't know what you and Mrs. Travers were doing at the library?"

"We were researching places in the area to visit while Mrs. Travers was recuperating from her concussion."

"Why the library?" Hill asked. "There are several visitor bureaus up and down I-80."

"It's a great place to do research," Jackson said. "I've used libraries often in my life, both personally and in business. You should try it sometime."

"To that point, Mr. King, why did you send Mrs. Travers back into the library before the ambulance came?"

"To get our belongings." Jackson flinched when the needle hit a sensitive spot. "By the way, detective, did you ever discover if Lester was his first or last name?"

"His full name is Lester Lee Smith," Hill said. "We also checked out your paint splotch theory on Lester's pants with painting contractors and painters in the area. No one could recall ever seeing a person by Lester's description before he shaved into his disguise."

"The paint angle seemed logical. Good thing I didn't go into law enforcement, huh?"

"Actually, I believe you would make a damn good detective, Mr. King. Back to my original question, was your research in the library successful? Did you decide where you and Mrs. Travers are going to visit next?"

Touché. Jackson had changed the subject and Hill had not so subtly returned to it.

"We have a good idea where we might be heading next," Jackson answered.

"And where would that be, Mr. King?"

"Back to the hotel," Jackson said. "Mrs. Travers isn't over her concussion. And I know from experience in an hour or two the pain shots will wear off."

"If I haven't made myself perfectly clear, I will now," the detective said. "There is a missing link to this case you're not sharing with me. If I find either one of you withholding evidence, I will throw the book at you even if I have to re-edit the book."

Hill stomped out of the room. The doctor began stitching Jackson's arm. At least the person threatening him this time was on the right side of the law.

"Jackson King, what did you negotiate with Lester?" Dani demanded.

"Rather than a full-scale negotiation, it was a simple barter."

"What did you barter? Jackson?"

"Your life for Dalton's key," he said.

"You mean to tell me Lester only settled for the key? What else did you offer, Jackson?"

"I'll tell you some other time when you are in a better mood."

CHAPTER TWENTY-EIGHT

The clock's LED red numbers illuminated 2:19 a.m. Jackson was lying awake on his back in the darkness of his hotel bedroom. If he had dozed at all it couldn't have been for long. The left side of his body throbbed with an annoying soreness the same way it had the night after his first emergency room visit.

Dani had won last night's pain pill debate regarding who should distribute his medicine. She was concerned he would take more than what was prescribed on the label if the full vial was left on the nightstand. Smart lady; she was aware of his addictive nature.

In spite of his discomfort and lack of sleep, he felt fortunate. The showdown at the library yesterday with Lester could have been a disaster if Dani had been physically re-injured. How much would she suffer psychologically after being abducted? Thus far she appeared to be all right. Another concern was Lester eluding the police once again.

A slight flow of air in the room made Jackson's eyelids lift to their normal position. The breeze didn't come from an inactive air conditioner or heater. He held his breath waiting for his ears to tell him what his eyes couldn't. He detected a slight movement. Or maybe his imagination was working overtime? He reached for the lamp switch on the nightstand. A hand gripped his wrist to stop him.

"Sorry if I woke you, Jackson," Dani said in a tender tone. "I was leaving your next scheduled pain pill on the nightstand with a bottle of water."

"Thank you," Jackson puffed out. "You didn't wake me. I hope you didn't set the alarm in your room to bring me my pill."

"Actually, I did set the alarm, but it didn't matter. I couldn't sleep. Maybe I was worried I'd miss the time your next pill was due. Or maybe it was something the great philosopher Dr. Seuss had once said."

"Come on, Dani. I appreciate your concern, but I can take care of myself. You're not over your concussion. It's important you get as much quality sleep as you can." Jackson couldn't see the expression on her face. "Funny you should mention Dr. Seuss, though. He has always been a favorite of mine. Didn't know Theodor Seuss Geisel was a great philosopher. What did he say?"

"I'll tell you some other time, maybe as a reward for being a good patient."

She sat on the bed next to Jackson's uninjured right side and placed a tiny pill into his hand, followed by the bottled water. He swallowed the pill with two gulps, wiped a hand over his mouth, and allowed his head to plop back onto the pillow.

"Now, close your eyes." She put the bottle on the nightstand. "Are they closed?"

"Yes, but closing my eyes at this point isn't going to help me fall asleep. I'm only doing it because I want to know what Dr. Seuss said."

"Oh shush." She gently massaged his temples with her soft fingertips. "My daddy used to do this for me when I was a child and it worked every time. His strong hands were as tough as leather, but so soothing and reassuring. He would hum a song or tell me why he loved me so much. I don't know how he did it, but he always managed to come up with a different reason for loving me." Her voice quivered. "I still miss him. Guess I always will. He made me feel so special. It's the same feeling I get when I'm with you."

She softly kissed his cheek.

* * * * *

The clock beamed 7:10 a.m. Jackson blinked several times to make sure he was observing the correct time. Almost five hours of uninterrupted sleep. Darkness flooded the bedroom, but not from night. The drawn curtains blocked the start of the day's light. He couldn't recall ever sleeping in this late, even in the era of his nighttime imbibing and waking up with morning hangovers. Dani's soothing massage had worked wonders.

His left side ached, yet for some reason he was content to loll in between the sheets. He had always considered lying awake in bed a sign of laziness. There were only so many hours in a day to be productive. But now he marveled at how comfortable he was. He couldn't see if Dani had left another pill on the nightstand. The idea of stretching out and patting his hand on the stand for the miniscule white tablet made him hesitate. It would hurt like hell, but the pill might take some of the smarting edge off. What if he accidentally knocked the pill onto the carpet? Or if he lost his balance and fell onto the floor. He pictured in his mind a worse case scenario of Dani sprinting into the room in a panic to find her patient rolling around in fierce pain and stark naked.

It hurt every bit as Jackson expected after his hand reached the on/off switch at the base of the lamp. The shaded light made him squint. The bottle of water was there, but no pill. Maybe Dani forgot. Or better yet, maybe she overslept.

A slight movement in the bed made his eyelids jump to ready alert. He twisted around and found he wasn't alone. It shocked the pain out of him to see Dani fast asleep under the covers two feet away from him. Her relaxed, steady breathing suggested she was in a nice peaceful place. He marveled at her appealing features; the same beautiful way she looked when he first saw her asleep from the concussion in the hospital.

Jackson gritted his teeth and turned off the lamp. Now he knew why he was so content lounging in bed. His eyes closed. The pain pill would have to wait. He didn't want to disturb the sleep she so desperately needed. Nor did he want Dani to wake up and catch him streaking away from the bed, commando.

* * * * *

A few minutes before 9:00 a.m. Jackson propped a pillow against the headboard and eased up into a sitting position. He couldn't see Dani in the darkness, but it didn't matter as long as he knew she was there inches away from him.

At 9:47 Dani stirred. She drew in a breath through her nose and yawned. He switched on the lamp. Her eyes opened, blinking away the fog as she turned on the pillow to face him.

"Wh...What time is it? Dani asked in a husky voice.

"It's almost ten o'clock."

"In the morning?" Her voice cracked.

"In the morning," Jackson said. "You've been asleep for over seven hours. It's the first time you have slept this long since having the concussion - a good sign."

"Wow. I can't believe you're still in bed. You always get up so early. Did you get much sleep at all? Oh my God. I didn't give you your pain pills. Some nurse I am. How long have you been awake?"

"Not long."

"How are you feeling, Jackson?"

"The person who said a stitch in time saves nine wasn't talking about knife wounds." He smiled. "Actually all of my pain was alleviated by watching you sleep."

"I apologize." She ignored his flatter, threw off the sheet and blanket, exposing her white West Virginia Mountaineer's jersey and grey sweatpants. "I'll get your pill."

"Relax, Dani, I'm fine. The pill can wait."

They locked eyes for a second before she looked away.

"I bet you are wondering why I was sleeping in your bed?"

"Now that you mentioned it..."

"I can't believe I slept for so long. I should be embarrassed, but I'm not. Well, maybe a little." She sat on the sheet and crisscrossed her legs. "You fell asleep right away, but I didn't want to leave you. Since my sleep pattern lately has been in short increments, I figured if I did fall asleep, I would wake up before you did, and you would never know the difference. I was out as soon as my head hit the pillow."

"First time I've ever enjoyed lying awake in bed. Even fell back asleep. Maybe your lapse was a godsend, Dani. We may have discovered a perfect way for both of us to get a full night's sleep."

"I must look a fright, like one of those women in horror films." Dani gave him a shy look, ran a hand through her short brunette hair and peered at the open door.

Jackson held back a smile. He had never heard her be concerned about her appearance.

"Not a fright, Dani. More like a delight." He couldn't hold back his smile any longer. "I can't wait to tell Rose we slept together."

"Don't you dare, Jackson." She started to pinch his arm, but thought better of it. "Rose would never forgive you. Or me."

"Okay, okay. It will have to be our little secret."

"Rose doesn't know you were re-injured," Dani said. "What should I tell her?"

"Tell her we will be gone for a few more days, unless we get lucky. There are a lot of miles between Rocklin and Colfax, but we're close, Dani. I can feel it. I doubt we'll have to worry about Lester anymore. The police have probably captured him by now."

A good news - bad news scenario. If the police arrested Lester, Jackson and Dani were no longer in danger. How long would it take Detective Hill to badger Lester into telling him about Dalton's hidden duffle bag? Whether Jackson felt physically up to it or not, they had to find the padlock to Dalton's key and get out of Dodge.

"I have to admit," she said, "I was frightened when Lester grabbed me and tied me up with tape. But I didn't doubt for one second you would find a way to rescue me."

"Thanks for the vote of confidence. It was luck. Lester got greedy and made a mistake."

"I forgot." Dani put both hands on her hips. "You can't accept a compliment. What else did you barter with Lester besides Dalton's padlock key to get me back, Jackson?"

"I gave Lester a choice," Jackson said. "He could have Dalton's key and either your blonde wig or me. I figured it would be a tough choice since he shaved his head."

Dani laughed. A laugh Jackson had come to treasure. She put a finger to her lips and placed it on his lips.

"There was no wig in that negotiation," she said in a confident tone. "I'll get your pill."

"Good idea." Jackson pulled the top sheet to his bare chest. "And Dani, please take your time."

CHAPTER TWENTY-NINE

J ackson palmed a bill with Andrew Jackson's image folded into a square and placed it in the hotel bellman's hand after he carried and loaded their luggage into the trunk of his car. The young man's eyes blinked twice when he peeked at the tip before pocketing it. Three happy souls; one person elated to be twenty dollars richer, and two people on their way to search for the valuables taken from them years ago.

The more Jackson moved the better his stitched wounds felt. Dani had offered him a pain pill before they left their room, but he refused. This time, he would take extra precaution not to revisit the familiar and unfriendly confines of the hospital emergency room.

Jackson first drove to a locksmith's shop located in a mom-and-pop business section the bellman had recommended. A bell above the door clanged as they entered. Scent of oil-based machinery caught Jackson's nose. A young man with long sideburns and wearing a Sacramento River Cats' black and red baseball hat fronted hundreds of key blanks hanging on the wall. A smirk appeared on the locksmith's lips when he eyed the gold key Jackson held between his forefinger and thumb.

"The key you are holding goes to a Sturdee Padlock number A77." The locksmith slid a blue padlock to Jackson with an inserted gold key exactly like the one he was showing. "There are seven different colored A77 Sturdee Padlocks. We don't sell a lot of them, but they're well made. How many keys do you want me to cut?"

"Just one." Jackson handed him the key on the chain. "Are there many gold plated padlock keys in this shape and color?"

"Not to my knowledge and I've been in this business since I was eight years old. My granddaddy opened this shop; my daddy took it over, and now it's my turn. The key does have a weird shape... like a martini glass with ridges."

"Are you sure there isn't a way to find the lock color our key goes to?" Dani asked.

"Positive, Ma'am." The locksmith went to a station in the corner to cut the key.

Jackson bounced the blue Sturdee Padlock in his palm and found it to be heavier than most padlocks. Dani had asked a good question. It would have been a big advantage for them to be able to identify the lock they were searching for by color, but at least they were now armed with a sample of the shape and size of Dalton's lock.

It took the locksmith less than a minute to cut a new key. Jackson also purchased the blue Sturdee lock that came with a set of two keys. He inserted Dalton's original key into his A77. The notched metal slid in perfectly, but it wouldn't turn.

"You've been a big help." Jackson said, to the locksmith. "I have one last question, although you may find it is a bit off the wall. Have you ever seen a man in these parts with two different colored eyes?"

"No, sir. But I know a guy who owns a dog with two different eye colors. Didn't know it happened to humans."

Jackson guided his car onto Highway 80. Twenty-five minutes later they entered the city limits of Rocklin. Using the Rocklin yellow page he swiped from the library phonebook as a guide, they stopped at a gas station and received directions to the town's only public storage facility. The moment Jackson viewed the front of U-Stow & Go Mini Storage, he realized their search would be more difficult than he had thought. In order to gain access through the metal gate guarding the storage units, they would need the keypad code.

A woman with short, dyed red hair greeted them from her desk behind the counter when they entered the office. Rouge dominated her cheeks. Fried bacon aroma emanating from the apartment connected to the office made Jackson's stomach rumble even though they had breakfast at the hotel before leaving. Dani placed the blue lock onto the counter with the set of keys.

"How can I help you folks today?" The woman moved to the counter.

"Have you seen locks like this, maybe in a different color, on any of your units?"

"Can't say that I have. Can't say that I haven't."

"Would you mind if we walked the grounds and checked?" Jackson asked.

"Not at all," the woman said. "First you have to rent a unit."

"We'd be interested in your smallest unit for a brief period of time," Jackson said.

"Our five by five units are the smallest we have. It's more expensive if you rent for a month; which is our minimum."

"We will take the five by five for a month."

She pushed a form across the counter for Jackson to fill out. His stomach crooned again.

"Sorry about the aroma," the woman said. "My husband moonlights as a bartender at night. I keep telling him how his bacon and eggs breakfast affects the customers, but it falls on deaf ears." She smiled at Dani. "Do you have the same problem with your man?"

"Not at all. He's a good listener and he has my vote if there is ever a 'Mr. Considerate' contest." Dani tilted closer to the woman. "You have to train them right from the start."

Jackson cleared his throat. He finished the paper work by signing his name and handed the woman his credit card. She jotted a few words on the form, swiped his card, and handed it back along with a receipt.

"How long have you and your husband been managers here?" Jackson asked.

"Going on two years, but we've been in the business for over fifteen years."

"For the sake of asking, have you ever run across a man with two different colored eyes?"

"I would've remembered seeing a man with different colored eyes." She turned to a doorway. "Percy, you ever seen a man in these parts with eyes a different color?"

"Is this one of your damn riddles? Is he a Siamese twin?"

"Never mind. Sorry folks. He's always grouchy in the morning. Probably because he drinks more as bartender than he pours for his customers." She presented Jackson with paperwork copies, the four digit code for the fence, and a layout of the unit locations. "Your five by five storage unit is located here at the red X. Once you get past the gate turn left, then turn right. Your unit is at the end on the left hand side."

Back in their car, Jackson buzzed down his driver's side window, punched a key pad on a pole, and waited for the gate to roll open. He drove to their storage unit and they split up. Dani walked to the left, Jackson to the right. They met back at their unit ten minutes later. Dani found three Sturdee locks. The key fit, but it wouldn't turn. Jackson located one, with the same result. One storage facility down, dozens more to go.

Jackson headed off the beaten path of Highway 80 onto Route 65 to travel to the cities of Whitney and Lincoln. Their findings were the same. Two hours later, they were back on Highway 80 seeking public storage sites in the towns of Loomis, Penryn, and Newcastle. Only one storage facility produced a possibility. A sign on the gate indicated the office would be closed until tomorrow due to a funeral. Customers who had the code number still had access their units. On their way back, they would return to this storage facility if unsuccessful in finding Dalton's duffel bag.

By the time they approached the town of Auburn, darkness was closing in. It had been a long, unproductive day. Dani had turned quiet. She didn't complain, but she appeared fatigued. Perhaps a headache was plaguing her? Or maybe doubt was creeping in.

He parked in front of a large white two story house surrounded by groomed hedges and red, white, and blue flowers. A "Royal Inn" sign stood centered in the middle of the lawn.

"What is the Royal Inn?" Dani asked.

"A bed and breakfast. The Royals are friends of mine. Haven't seen them in a long time."

The features of the man behind the check-in counter brightened when he saw Jackson enter through the front door. After giving Jackson a hardy handshake with two hands, he called for his wife. She came into the lobby, screamed her delight, and hugged Jackson.

"And who is this pretty lady?" she asked, leaving Jackson to shake Dani's hand.

"Roy and Linda Royal, please meet Dani Travers. She's an associate of mine."

"The Royals and a King." Dani laughed. "I feel out of place."

"Even if Jackson's last name wasn't King, he's regal to us," Linda said. "We wouldn't be in business if it wasn't for him."

"Linda and Roy have a tendency to exaggerate at times," Jackson said. "But that doesn't make them bad people."

"Exaggerate my patoot." Linda wiggled a forefinger at him. "Jackson saved us from going under. We had to close our doors because of a major plumbing problem. This man loaned us money and provided free advertising on his billboards when we re-opened."

Jackson held up a hand. "You're going to give Dani the wrong impression about me."

"If you haven't noticed, Mr. King has a difficult time accepting compliments," Dani said.

"What brings you to Old Town Auburn, Jackson?" Roy hitched a thumb to a jean pocket.

"Dani and I are working our way up Highway 80 on a project. We need two rooms for the night. I don't think she has stayed in a bed and breakfast before." He removed a credit card from his wallet. "I think she would enjoy the experience of your great hospitality."

Roy pushed the card back. "Don't you dare embarrass us by trying to pay, Jackson King."

"I wish you would have called ahead of time, Jackson." Linda's eyes zeroed in on Dani.

"We only have one room available. But you are certainly welcome to it if..."

"Please, Linda, one room is fine," Dani smiled. "Don't worry; I'm sure Jackson won't mind sleeping on a cot."

Linda and Roy exchanged a glance, before staring at Jackson. Jackson, in turn, gazed at Dani.

"I'm kidding." Dani laughed. "Your inn is so beautiful. I love the way you have decorated with lovely antiques and paintings. You have such a great eye for colors. Please give me the grand tour, Linda. How long has the inn been in existence? What inspired you? When did you and Roy meet Jackson?"

"Slow down, Dani," Linda said, putting her arm through Dani's arm. "We have all evening. The first thing you should be aware of, you are the first woman Jackson has ever brought to our inn."

CHAPTER THIRTY

Jackson ran a palm over the green felt poker table. Dani shuffled Jackson's baseball cards as if they were a regular deck of playing cards. He cautioned her to be careful not to bend the cards out of shape. Dani told him to shush and served out the first card from the top of the deck to him face down. He carefully peeked at his card so she couldn't see what he had. It took every bit of restraint for Jackson to keep a poker face. Dani had dealt him the Honus Wagner American Tobacco card, the most valuable baseball card ever printed. A second look eliminated his euphoria. Honus was wrinkled, creased, bent, and ripped, taking away most of the sentimental and dollar value from the card.

Jackson woke up with a start. He was lying on his back. His left leg and arm ached. A crazy nightmare, although his watch on the nightstand said it was seven fifteen in the morning. Unbelievable. They overslept again.

Dani was lying next to his undamaged right side. Her pillow had shifted from the other side of the bed to unite against his. She was facing him, peaceful in slumber with a hand on his arm. Jackson's eyes closed, content this was not a dream.

＊ ＊ ＊ ＊ ＊

The egg, sausage, waffle, and country fried potato breakfast was fit for a king, his lady, and other Royal guest subjects. It wasn't only the scrumptious meal that put Jackson in an upbeat mood. He couldn't think of a better way to start a day than to have Dani sleeping next to him. Nor could he control pulsing psychic signals; a feeling that rarely failed him. This was the day they would find the storage unit housing Dalton's duffle bag.

After their meal, Jackson called the office from their room to speak to Rose and Kenny. He got the impression his trusted employees were enjoying their upgraded positions of authority to run his business. He was in no hurry to get back to work - a first for him.

On their way out, Dani presented the Royals with a cartoon sketch image of themselves standing in front of the inn by their sign. Their smiles portrayed how thrilled they were with her gift. Roy and Linda escorted them to the car.

Jackson sucked in Auburn's invigorating morning air. Frost had turned the lawn white, reminding him of West Virginia. Overhead, a lonely puffy cloud dominated a vibrant blue sky; a perfect day to end their search with the grand prize. He assumed his position behind the steering wheel, buzzed down his window, and peered up at the Royals.

"Have you ever seen a man in these parts with two different colored eyes?"

"That condition is called heterochromia," Linda said. "One iris is a different color than the other. A schoolmate of mine had it. But I've never seen a man with it."

"Heterochromia." Jackson started the car after the Royals returned to the inn. "Who knew?" Dani placed her fingers on his hand before he could shift.

"What if we don't find Dalton's storage unit?" she asked. "What if your padlock key premise is wrong? What if the duffle bag and the articles he stole are no longer in existence? Then what, Jackson?"

"I'm confident we will find what we are looking for."

"And if we don't, what about your business?"

"Rose and Kenny have everything under control."

"Whatever happened to the incurable workaholic?" she asked.

"He's on a mission."

Dani removed her hand from his and gazed out the side window. Maybe she didn't share his belief about finding the duffle bag. Or was something else bothering her?

Three of the five storage facilities from the Auburn yellow page list were located on or right off Highway 49 towards Grass Valley and Nevada City. Eleven Star Public Storage was their first stop. They entered through the pedestrian gate and found a man on a ladder with a sheet of sandpaper in his hand. The office white side wall and teal eave were in need of a new coat of paint. Sitting on the ground were paint cans, paintbrushes, sandpaper, rollers, trays, and a drop cloth.

"Good morning," Jackson said, staring up at the man. "Are you the manager here?"

"Guilty. If you need to rent a space, the wife will take care of you inside the office." He tilted his hat back. "I don't even know if this is the right grade of sandpaper."

"I take it you're not much of a painter," Dani said.

"The only brush I'm comfortable using is for my teeth. The painter I hired up and left us before finishing. Didn't even try to collect what we owed him. Now I know why his bid was so much cheaper than the rest."

"The name of the painter you hired wouldn't happen to be Lester, would it?"

"Yea. Yea. The guy's name is Lester. You know him?"

"Well enough to say the probability of his coming back to finish the job is like nil."

Dani questioned Jackson with her eyes. He first pointed to the cans of white and teal paint, then his jeans. She nodded her understanding. How ironic would it be if Lester was working at the self-storage facility Dalton used to store the duffle bag?

"Sir, you might want to use a coarser grade of sandpaper," Dani said, waving a sheet.

"Thanks, Ma'am." He stepped down two rungs and grabbed the sheet from Dani.

"Would you mind if we examined the different types of locks on your storage units?"

"Are you doing some kind of study?" The man's head bobbed when he produced a better result with the new sandpaper sheet.

"Very astute of you," Jackson said. "Our project is to ascertain how many customers use a particular lock."

"Well if it ain't a Master Lock, you won't find many of what you're looking for." The manager stopped rubbing. "I'm not supposed to let anybody in if they ain't renting." He looked down at Dani. "Would it be better to paint the wall first or the trim?"

"The trim," Dani answered. "You might want to get a paint sprayer for the wall."

"Thank you, Ma'am. You and your partner go right ahead."

They walked eight rows; one hundred and forty units to a row, depending on the size of the units. Over ninety percent of the locks were Master Locks and zero percent were Strudee, verifying what the manager deduced.

"The good news is," Jackson said, on the way back to the car, "our quest would have taken weeks if Dalton chose a Master Lock to store his stash."

Back on the road, Jackson turned off Highway 49 and drove up a hill to the second public storage facility. They were greeted by a friendly husband and wife team inside the office sitting at opposite desks. The wife's desktop was piled with papers. The husband was reading a *Sports Illustrated* magazine.

"How large of a storage unit were you looking for?" the wife asked.

"For the time being, a five by five for a month," Jackson said.

Dani placed the blue Sturdee lock on the counter. She leaned her head on Jackson's shoulder, breathing hard through her mouth.

"I'm a bit woozy from the drive." Dani blinked at the woman. "Would you mind if I got some air by walking the flat unit grounds while you conduct business?"

"You do look pale, dear," the wife said, pointing to a side door. "You go right ahead. This altitude often gets to our visitors."

By the time Dani returned, Jackson had learned how the husband and wife met, the names of their kids and grandkids, and every public storage facility they ever managed.

"Are you feeling better, dear?" the wife asked. "Your cheeks have more color."

"A bit." Dani pinned fingers to her temple. "Thanks for asking. Jackson, can we return to rent the storage unit at another time? I'd like to go back to the inn so I can lie down?"

Jackson apologized to the managers and led Dani to the car.

"A very convincing performance," he said. "What did you discover, if anything?"

"I found one Sturdee lock. But the key wouldn't turn, just like the others. Truthfully, I wasn't acting, Jackson. Maybe it is the altitude."

"We'll go back to the inn so you can rest," he said.

"Let's finish what we started." She opened the passenger door.

Two of the three remaining Auburn public storage facilities didn't produce a single Sturdee lock. The office of the third storage was temporarily closed for thirty minutes, thus putting another facility on the return list. Dani's frown showed her disappointment. For Jackson, however, Colfax had always been the most logical place for Dalton to store the duffle bag.

The Mercedes headed up Highway 80 to Colfax. Dani's eyes were fixed on patches of snow hugging the roadside fronting a denseness of tall trees. The temperature lowered. Jackson switched on the heat to warm the inside of the car and Dani's mood.

Jackson took the Colfax turnoff and parked at the curb in front of a convenience store/ gas station. A "For Rent" sign was on the closed auto repair garage door.

"And we are stopping here because..." Dani said, before they entered the store.

"The Blake family owns the property. Mrs. Blake - Mama to everyone - and her kids operate the store and gas pumps. The family has been in Colfax forever. They lease out the garage; cars have a tendency to break down right around here. We can get directions to Colfax Storage and the best cup of coffee in town."

"Mr. King," the boy behind the counter bellowed. "I don't know if you remember me. I'm LeRoy. Mama is finally letting me work behind the counter when I'm not in school."

"Sure I remember you, LeRoy. You've grown and your voice has changed." Jackson nudged Dani's elbow. "This is Mrs. Travers. Could we please get two cups of your great coffee - one black and one with cream - and directions to Colfax Storage?"

Dani snooped around while LeRoy poured. The store was small in size, but almost any item a traveler would need was strategically placed in racks, shelves, or hanging. Jackson had met Mama years ago when she inquired about leasing a billboard. It was obvious she was a shrewd businesswoman. Her little enterprise was a literal goldmine, plus she owned other properties in the area.

"Two cups of coffee on the house, Mr. King." LeRoy placed the cups with plastic lids on the counter. "As far as directions, take the overpass into town and then the first left for a quarter mile. Colfax Storage has a big sign. You can't miss it. Tell the manager you're a friend of Mama's; they'll give you a better rate."

"LeRoy, have you ever seen a man with different colored eyes around town?"

"Nah. Most of the adults I see in these parts wear sunglasses 'cause they work outside."

Dani gave LeRoy a thumb's up when she sipped her coffee.

"Tell Mama and your sister LeAnn hello for me." Jackson slapped a five spot on the counter for the coffees and jammed another five into the boy's shirt pocket.

"Thanks, Mr. King." Leroy produced a toothy smile and patted his pocket. "Mama will be sorry she missed you. She's in Auburn buying an ad in the Journal for the garage. You'd be surprised how much business that garage brings into the store."

"It pays to advertise, LeRoy." Jackson opened the door for Dani.

CHAPTER THIRTY-ONE

ive minutes after leaving the convenience store, the Mercedes was parked in front of Colfax Storage. Excitement buzzed through Jackson's whole body as they walked through the pedestrian gate leading to the office; a sensation he often experienced before cutting major deals. The office front was adorned with colorful plants and trimmed bushes encased in a brick flower box. They were greeted by a husband and wife manager team when Jackson opened the door for Dani.

"Welcome," the wife said. "You came to the right place if you're looking for storage."

"Mama from the convenience store sent us here." Jackson extended a hand to pet a tiny dog resting on a chair in front of the counter. "We have a rather strange request. If you would please give us five minutes, there is a story we would like to share with you."

"What are you selling?" the heavyset husband asked in a stiff tone.

"Nothing that will cost you or your business one penny. But with your permission you could help dozens of people who have been abused. Five minutes is all we ask. If I fail to convince you, I will pay you for your time."

"That's some sales pitch." The husband leaned back in his chair. "Give it your best shot."

Jackson proceeded to tell the couple about their mission, including how Dalton Peppers stole prized items from his victims. Dani held up the blue Sturdee lock when Jackson mentioned the locksmith. The wife had tears in her eyes when Jackson finished.

"You said this Dalton dude has different colored eyes." The husband scratched his chin.

"Right." Dani said. "One blue and one brown."

"I've seen him a couple of times, but not lately." The husband rose to his feet.

"Did you see Dalton here?" Jackson asked.

"Nope. I saw him playing pool at a downtown Colfax bar. Skinny guy. He wore shaded glasses. I noticed them eyes when he cleaned the lenses with a hanky."

"We learned Dalton lived somewhere in Colfax." Jackson held up the gold key. "More than ever, I believe he stored the duffle bag here at this facility. We understand you are bound by rules and regulations. Rather than deceiving you as renters, all we are asking is for you to allow us to inspect the units for the Sturdee lock that fits this key."

"My stomach's a churnin' for both of you," the wife said. "What are you gonna do if that key opens the lock and you find the duffle bag?"

"One, we want to reclaim what Dalton Peppers stole from us," Dani said. "Picture frames my father gave to me before he died and Jackson's childhood baseball card collection. Two, we will try to find the other victims Dalton molested and return their valuables to them." She lifted Jackson's camera hanging from her neck. "In good faith, we would want either one of you to go with us to verify inventory found in the duffle bag."

"You sold me." The husband made eye contact with his wife. "I'll go with you."

The manager followed Jackson and Dani in a golf cart to the far end of the property. Same routine, different storage facility. Jackson found a brown Strudee Lock securing a unit's metal door in the third row. He winked at Dani before inserting the key, but it wouldn't turn. Dani's head dropped.

Jackson moved on without saying a word. In the fourth row they passed a short man with a mustache unloading boxes of casino coupons from a hand truck. Three metal doors down, Jackson stopped at an orange Sturdee Lock. He inserted the key without hesitation. Same result. Jackson charged ahead, undaunted. *Putt-putt* sounded from the golf cart following them to the next row.

They entered the last row with Jackson leading. Once more, Master was the dominant lock. Halfway down the row a red Sturdee Lock stood out like a radiated flag. Jackson's arm and leg were pain free, compliments of what he anticipated finding behind the door.

"Do you want to do the honors, Dani?" Jackson touched the lock, then stepped away.

Dani edged up to the unit's ridged metal door with the gold key the locksmith had cut. Her hand trembled. She inserted the key into the bottom of the base and looked up at the sky. Her fingers applied pressure. The key didn't budge.

* * * * *

The altitude in Colfax had nothing to do with the mounting pressure attacking Jackson as he led Dani down the public storage office's cement walkway towards the car. If they were on a sports team, one teammate would give him a stank-eye signifying he screwed up big time to lose the game. Another teammate might pat him on the ass and tell him to shake it off. Dani's silence would be the most gut-wrenching by far.

A screeching black cat skittered past them in a blur. Dani reacted by bumping into his side. The lesions on his leg and arm screamed as he gritted his teeth. The cat disappeared and hid in an expanse of green shrubbery. He opened Dani's passenger door and waited for her to get settled. The long walk around the rear of his car wasn't nearly long enough.

"I'm sorry, Dani." Jackson slid behind the steering wheel. "It troubles me to no end I failed you. More than anything I wanted to help find the frames your proud father gave to you. It's not my nature to give up. If we have to start over again, so be it."

"Are you admitting the great Jackson King is fallible?" Dani eyed the gold key in her palm. "I wouldn't be honest if I told you I'm not disappointed, but you didn't let me down, Jackson. On the contrary, you are my hero - right up there with my Daddy. I truly believe if *you* can't find where Dalton stored our valuables, no one else can either."

"I'm no hero." He offered a weak smile. "And maybe I'm out of my element here, but I'd hate to throw in the towel, or in this case Dalton's key. Wish I could figure out where I went wrong. It's possible one of the storage facilities we couldn't get into has the duffle bag. What I'm saying, Dani, we haven't lost yet."

"Jackson, we didn't lose. Don't you realize your baseball cards and my frames were the connection to an even greater treasure?"

"And what would that treasure be?" He turned to face her with his left hand tapping the steering wheel.

"We found each other."

Jackson gripped the wheel. Four insightful words. They never would have met without the link to Dalton.

"As you know," Dani continued, "Rose doesn't let the grass grow when she has something on her mind. She cut right to the essential issue about how much you changed in the past year, coupled with how different you are since I entered the scene. With all due respect to Rose, I didn't buy it when she said you were smitten - her word not mine. Rose pointed out how attentive and protective you are with me. How you shared your most valuable asset with me - your time. You even let Yogi live with me."

"Rose has a tendency to jump to conclusions and read into matters—"

She leaned over and kissed him softly on the lips, then pulled away before he could respond in kind.

"I always thought hate was the most powerful emotion I would ever feel," she said. "Yet the hate I had for Dalton doesn't compare to the deep affection I feel for you, Jackson. Being in love is a wonderful feeling, but it's also overwhelming as well as terrifying."

"I don't ever want you to be afraid of me." he said. "Rose was spot on. She understood how I felt about you before I did. I could never express that emotion because I didn't want you to feel pressured. And I still don't."

"It's not *you* I am afraid of, Jackson. It's *me*." She placed a hand on her chest. "I want to be able to reciprocate in all ways, but I can't assure a response that would satisfy you."

"You've made me overly aware of the one thing I lacked in my life, Dani: contentment. The time we have spent together fulfilled that need."

"Contentment, but for how long, Jackson?" Dani took his hand into hers. "How long will it take for your contented bliss to turn into discontent? You are the master achiever, whether it's personal or business. You deal with a project or a mission, conquer it successfully, and move on to the next challenge. It's opposite for me. I have always pushed men away - and a few women friends too - who wanted to get close to me. Our histories don't jive very well."

"Let's create new history, Dani. The connection we share is real. But it's not like I can offer you a lifetime guarantee. Nor do your emotions come with a warranty. Let's take it slow and *trust* in our feelings for each other."

"It's not that easy, Jackson. At least not for me. With all of my heart I want to start a new life with you, but at what cost? I could never forgive myself for making your life miserable - been there, done that, failed miserably. You have totally ignored your business because of me. I keep wondering if our fairytale romance is too good to be true. Or even real." Dani swallowed hard. "What I'm trying to say is, I need to sort things out away from you. I think it would be best for me to go back to West Virginia. If I return, it will be for good."

Heaviness invaded Jackson's chest, making it difficult to breathe. The last thing he expected was Dani running away from him. Fear haunting Dani her whole life was rearing its ugly head and manipulating her once again. He couldn't help Dani overcome her trepidation unless she first conquered it herself. For a man who had made a fortune making deals, this was one transaction he couldn't close because it wouldn't be best for Dani.

"I have always been a believer in keeping an open door. For you, Dani, that door represents my heart. I understand why you have reservations. Conversely, I have none. Take all the time you need. From my point of view, I don't see anything wrong with a fairytale romance when it's real and right. In time, I *trust* you will come around to the same conclusion. You once asked me if we were partners. I said yes, partners on the same team. While there is no 'i' in team, there is 'us' in *trust*."

CHAPTER THIRTY-TWO

Jackson positioned himself on the south end of Marie's green couch as usual. He removed a string of Yogi's hair from his dark slacks. The books in the bookcase appeared to be in the same order. Wall art had not changed. Knick-knacks were where they should be. Marie was sporting a blue outfit he had seen before, and her short silver hairdo was set the same way. Yet, everything felt different.

"It has been awhile since our last session, Jackson." Marie placed her glasses on a notepad. "I noticed a slight limp when you walked in. Did you hurt yourself?"

Jackson produced a deflated laugh. Marie asked a double-edged question. The wounds were an annoyance now, but Dani's absence had become a deep ache. He started to cross his stitched leg, and thought better of it. Instead, he leaned back into the couch and relayed the events of the last three weeks, beginning with how they nailed Richard Ransom; located Dalton Peppers, matched wits with Lester, went on a public storage hunt, fell in love, and ended with Rose delivering Dani to the San Francisco airport.

"My goodness." Marie glanced at her notes. "Your three week escapade with Dani was like an action-packed adventure movie."

"I'm not too crazy about the ending."

"The ending is still up in the air. How are you dealing with Dani returning to West Virginia?"

"I equate it to getting sober and trying to fill an irreplaceable void. In terms of days, we didn't spend a long time together, yet in that span we were inseparable. It was a closeness I've never experienced before. I'm trying not to think what my life will be like without Dani if she decides to stay in West Virginia. Hell, even my dog Yogi is bummed out."

"Have you talked to Dani since Rose drove her to the airport?"

"No, but I'm assuming Rose has." Jackson peered down at the rug. "When I asked Rose, she got snippy with me and said it was none of my business. I think - no I'm pretty damn sure - Rose blames me for Dani leaving."

"You said Dani needed time away from you to make a decision. What was your initial reaction when she told you she was going back to West Virginia?"

"Shock!" He shook his head. "It was totally unexpected. Dani said our relationship was overwhelming and terrifying. I fully get that. She was fearful I would become disenchanted with her because of my history. And she was worried she wouldn't be capable of being a satisfying partner."

"Those are significant concerns for someone who has had a lifetime of self-esteem issues."

He cocked his head to the side. "Damn it, Marie. Everything I've worked for means nothing to me without Dani. Are you trying to say you wouldn't recommend a relationship between two people who were molested as kids?"

"I'm not saying that at all, Jackson. It may work out fine. Both of you are fortunate to have found each other and to experience healthy feelings of love. It's natural for Dani to be fearful. And it is your nature to be upbeat about moving onto new objectives. Have you considered calling her or flying to West Virginia?"

"You bet," he said. "But if I contact Dani it might be counterproductive. She needs space. She knows how I feel about her and those feeling aren't going to change. I want to help her. I want to be there for her if she will let me."

"Do you think not finding Dalton's duffle bag is another reason Dani left?"

"You would have to ask Dani. I want to believe the outcome of our search had nothing to do with her decision. Then again, she did leave without our finding the frames."

"Are you blaming yourself for not finding Dani's frames?" Marie chewed on an end of her glasses. "Based on the information you had, which wasn't much, it seemed to be a near impossible task...even for you, Jackson."

"If you recall," Jackson said, "I entered into the deal with Dani thinking the very same thing. I can't help but believe we were close to finding what Dalton stole from us. I missed something, Marie. But for the life of me, I can't figure out what it is."

"Again, based on your history, if you did overlook something, Jackson, there is a good chance it will eventually come to you." She put her glasses back on and glanced at the clock. "I'm wondering, what were you feeling after you confronted Dalton Peppers in his hospital room?"

"I didn't get a chance to confront Dalton. In fact, I never would have recognized him and his different colored eyes from where I was positioned in the room. He had no idea who I was." Jackson ran a finger down the crease in his slacks. "To answer your question, I felt sorry for Dalton. He wanted to die in the worst way. I tried to save what time he had left. As it turned out, our being in the room led to his suicide."

"However, Lester was intent on murdering Dalton with or without knowledge of where Dalton hid his..." she looked down at her notes, "gold coins. The fact you felt sorrow for Dalton and tried to save him is quite something, Jackson. There was a time in your life where you couldn't have done that."

"I don't deserve kudos...*thank you, Dr Stiller.*"

Marie smiled. "At the library you recognized Lester from Dani's drawing. That in itself is amazing given Dani had no memory of seeing Lester."

"Dani is a pretty amazing person," Jackson said.

"Coming from an amazing man, that is high praise indeed."

"Thank you, Dr. Stiller."

"I meant that sincerely, Jackson. You have been blessed with a keen intuitive mind. Your descriptions guided Dani. But I'm having trouble understanding how you were so sure it was Lester sitting at the library table?"

"Lester was wearing the same paint-splotched jeans he wore at the hospital. I thought he might have been a painter, but the police pooh-poohed my theory after looking into it. We discovered later Lester did small painting jobs. Ironically, he was in the midst of painting a public storage office we visited."

"Therefore your painting insight was correct," Marie said.

"However, you were convinced the public storage in Colfax would produce Dalton's duffle bag, which up to this point has turned out to be off the mark. Are you having a difficult time admitting you could have been wrong?"

Jackson ran a hand through his hair. The gnawing in his stomach and mind wouldn't go away. Dalton's duffle bag was out there somewhere.

"To your point, Marie, I'm willing to own up to being wrong. When I am wrong, I want to know why so I won't make the same mistake. Look, Dalton told Lester the valuables he stole were in storage. From the gold key on Dalton's neck chain, we were able to figure out it belonged to a padlock that isn't widely used. Public storage units use padlocks. It made sense to me Dalton would store the bags near where he last lived and there is only one storage facility in Colfax."

"You are human, Jackson, whether you think you are or not. You have to admit there is a good possibility Dalton lied to Lester or disposed of the valuables years ago. Or he used another vehicle other than public storage. What was Dalton doing in Colfax?"

"I don't know." Jackson shrugged his shoulders. "Dalton came to California wanting to be... holy shit, that's it." Jackson jumped up. "Marie, you are a miracle worker."

"Thank you," she said. "If I was a real miracle worker, I would know how I worked a miracle. Will you please share with me why I have been elevated to such a prestigious status?"

"Yes, but not now. I will look forward to telling you the results of your genius at our next session."

Jackson shook her hand and tore from the office.

CHAPTER THIRTY-THREE

Less than three hours after Jackson sprinted from Marie's San Francisco office, he was standing with Mama's oldest daughter, LeAnn, in a small two-room apartment ogling a Sturdee Lock guarding a closet's contents. To Dalton Peppers, the closet was a storage unit. The lock's shank looped through a metal hasp attached to the wood door. Dalton had seven lock colors to choose from and selected a lock that had a plain metal finish. The same lock Jackson saw on Dalton's green duffle in the motel room.

Jackson fished Dalton's gold colored key and chain from his coat pocket. The room contained a twin bed, card table with two folding chairs, dresser, tiny refrigerator, plug-in heater, and TV with rabbit ears. A bathroom completed the apartment.

A bus horn beeped from the front of the convenience store; the driver's message for the passengers to return to the bus with their hot and cold drinks and bags of munchies. Many years ago, Mama nurtured her small business into a big moneymaker by steering bus traffic heading to Reno to make stops at her store.

The temperature outside was in the forties. The heater was off, but sweat snaked down Jackson's cheeks. LeAnn, holding Jackson's camera, was perspiring for another reason.

"We've known you for a long time, Mr. King. You've become a family friend. It takes a lot to earn Mama's trust. I have to tell you, being in this room kind of creeps me out. What are you expecting to find behind DJ's closet door? Nothing dead, I hope."

"I appreciate you helping me, LeAnn," Jackson said. "We would have known right away if there was something deceased in there."

Jackson smiled to reassure her. He had seen LeAnn blossom into a beautiful young lady; light brown skin, big puffy hair, a touch of makeup to enhance her striking dark eyes, and a killer smile. She was outgoing similar to her mother, brothers, and sisters.

"What I'm expecting to find is based on a theory," Jackson said.

"If my premise is correct, I'm going to need your assistance by taking pictures with my camera. Before we do that, though, what can you tell me about this DJ guy; starting with his full name?"

"He went by DJ," she said. "I don't think any of us knew his first or last name. He worked the garage for over two years. People say he was a good mechanic. He had his own tools; kept mostly to himself. He paid his rent on time and in cash. Over two months ago, DJ told Mama he was sick and would be gone for awhile. He never came back."

"I saw him several times when I stopped by to say hello to the family on my way to Reno," Jackson said. "But he was always working in that dark garage so I never got a good look at him. Did you notice anything different about his appearance? Specifically his eyes."

"DJ wore tinted glasses when he worked in the garage and sunglasses outside. I never saw him without a baseball cap pulled down low over his forehead. We thought he might be sensitive to light or the sun."

Jackson swiped sweat from his forehead with the back of a hand. If DJ was indeed Dalton Peppers, the J must be the first letter of his middle name. Maybe his eyes were sensitive to light; a good reason to wear tinted glasses or sunglasses as well as to hide odd colored eyes that could identify him. Was he even aware Lester or perhaps other victims he molested were seeking him for revenge?

"Did DJ live alone?" Jackson asked. "Or have many guests?"

"I think DJ lived alone. He wasn't a talkative person. I didn't pay much attention if he had visitors." She clutched the camera. "Should I take your picture in front of the closet?"

"Yes, but in stages that will tell the story of what we find behind the locked closet door."

Jackson stepped aside for LeAnn to snap photos. He moved to the closet. The camera lens followed him clicking away. Could LeAnn hear the loud beat thumping in his chest? The sixth-sense mojo he had always counted on had returned after going AWOL at the Colfax Public Storage. The duffle bag had to be in this closet.

Jackson blew out a nervous breath. His fingers' strangled

the lock's cold metal. The key slid into the bottom of the body, as expected. One righteous twist to the right could open new doors for Dani and maybe close the old ones. He applied pressure. The lock clicked open as LeAnn snapped another picture.

Jackson removed the lock from the hasp and yanked away the latch. A quick look over his shoulder revealed LeAnn's questioning eyes. Jackson twisted the doorknob and pulled the door open. LeAnn gasped. Jackson stepped back, before charging forward into the pitch dark closet. Something hit his forehead, stopping him cold. He tugged on the cord, illuminating an overhead light. LeAnn gasped again, louder. Two green duffle bags stood tall against the closet's back wall.

Jackson braced against the side closet wall to hold himself up. LeAnn had a hand over her mouth, most likely unsure what was in the duffle bags.

"Please sit down, LeAnn, so I can explain what this is all about." Jackson dragged one of the duffle bags from the closet, tilted it against the wall, and sat across from her at the table. "DJ, also known as Dalton Peppers, was a sick, perverted man. He died recently. Inside the duffle bags are sentimental mementos he stole from children he sexually molested. I'm one of them. Please take a picture of every item I remove from the bags for an inventory list. The goal is to return the items to the people Dalton violated."

"Mr. King, what did DJ take from you?" LeAnn wiped cheeks with a sweater sleeve.

"My entire baseball card collection packed into three cigar boxes. I'm also privy to the items he stole from a friend of mine; two picture frames holding a blue ribbon and a certificate of honor. And gold coins from another victim."

"I said a little prayer that we find them, Mr. King." She turned to the doorway. "But we are going to need more film. I'll get some rolls from the store."

"Hold on, LeAnn. It's a digital camera. It doesn't use film. You can keep snapping pictures. It's like a mini computer. Once you have taken an individual picture of every item I remove from the bag and place on the floor, take a shot of everything."

Jackson opened the duffle bag and removed a necklace made

with plastic beads. He held the necklace out for LeAnn to take a picture and placed it on the floor. Next, he pulled out a cap gun, followed by a puppet, yoyo, small trophy, ballet slippers, bag of marbles, toy soldiers, a doll, a teddy bear with an eye missing, and a piggy bank.

At the bottom of the duffle bag, Jackson dug out a pouch filled with gold coins. LeAnn held the camera down when he laughed out loud and poured the coins into his palm.

"A fanatical man named Lester was willing to kill to recover the gold coins his grandfather gave to him as a child. As you can see, they are not gold, nor are they coins. They're gold colored slugs. A cruel ruse a granddaddy played on his grandchild."

LeAnn snapped a picture of Lester's slugs and all the items on the floor. Jackson brought out the second bag. Many of the items were similar to those in the first bag as he laid them onto the floor. Jackson's heart jumped as if it was on a trampoline when his hand hit something familiar. He eased out three cigar boxes one at a time. Thirty-five year old memories floated in his head as he untied the string on one of the boxes. LeAnn's hand was on his shoulder when he lifted the lid. Encased in wax paper were his hall of fame baseball cards. Honus Wagner's American Tobacco card was on top of one of the stacks staring back at him.

"Praise the lord, Mr. King. I'm so happy for you."

Jackson was too emotional to speak. He re-tied the string and snuggled the boxes into a corner away from the other items. Back at the duffle bag, he removed a pocket knife, baseball mitt, and a pillowcase. Inside the pillowcase were two wood frames with glass covering a crayon drawing overlapped by a first place blue ribbon and a certificate of honor. Jackson held the frames against his chest. If only Dani was with him to enjoy this moment. If only Dani was with him, period. He placed the frames next to the cigar boxes.

"You found the cards, frames, and fake coins." She did a modest dance after taking pictures.

Heavy footsteps behind LeAnn made Jackson turn his head towards the doorway. Detective Hill marched into the room with a gun in one hand and his badge in the other.

"Jackson King. You are under arrest!"

CHAPTER THIRTY-FOUR

J ackson didn't bother to raise his hands up. LeAnn's brown eyes enlarged as Detective Hill stood next to her. He was wearing jeans, a red fleece jacket, and two days worth of whiskers. He had the look of a man who was working on his day off or on vacation.

"LeAnn Blake," Jackson said, "this is Detective Hill from the Sacramento Police Department. Detective, LeAnn has nothing to do with why I'm here."

"I'm aware of that, Mr. King," the detective said. "Miss Blake, you may go back to the store, but please leave the camera. Sorry if I frightened you. Say hey to Mama. I've known her for a long time. She's a lovely lady."

LeAnn's eyes went to Jackson. He signaled with a slight head bob it was okay for her to leave him. She handed the camera to the detective and left the room.

"Isn't the gun a tad overdramatic, detective?" Jackson asked.

"It depends, Mr. King. You didn't enter this building illegally, so your actions wouldn't be considered a burglary. But if you have been caught red-handed stealing someone else's property - property that doesn't belong to you, then it is a crime. Are you armed, Mr. King?"

"No, detective. What if the property is my own that was stolen from me?"

"Two steals don't make a right," the detective said, lifting the bottom of his jacket and holstering the gun. "Can you prove all of these stolen items are yours?"

Jackson peered at the three cigar boxes and Dani's frames in the corner of the room. He slid out a chair for the detective and settled in on the other folding chair. Hill unzipped his jacket, stepped over several items on the floor and sat across from Jackson.

"As an intelligent investigator you should have picked up on the fact LeAnn was taking pictures of each item to inventory what was in both duffle bags. Not exactly a thing a thief would do, right?" Jackson's hand slapped the table. "You didn't come all this way to arrest me for stealing anything, did you?"

"You are correct." Hill crossed his leg. "I was standing outside when you informed LeAnn why you came here. I assume the frames in the pillowcase were Mrs. Travers' property as a child. And the slugs were Lester's. I find your mission to return the items Dalton Peppers' stole from the children he molested quite commendable."

Jackson's head shot back. "Then why are you playing Colombo and arresting me?"

"You are under arrest because you withheld information and evidence from the police during an investigation."

"Oh, that." Jackson shrugged a shoulder. "I won't argue the point about withholding information. However, I didn't have the evidence at the times you questioned me."

"But you do now," Hill said, his lips spreading into a grin.

"Actually, I haven't taken them...yet. How did you find me?"

"From two sources," the detective said. "The librarian told me about the missing phonebook pages. You are damn lucky that woman isn't a judge because she would have sent you to San Quentin for life. The other source was Lester."

"You caught him?"

"The same day he ran from the library. Lester was vehement about you stealing all the items Dalton Peppers took from the people he violated. I followed the provocative trail you and Mrs. Travers left all the way up to Mama's store and Colfax Storage. The storage managers are big fans of yours and Mrs. Travers. By the way, where is she?"

"She went back home to another state." Jackson glanced at the frames.

"Lover's spat?"

"I wish it was that simple, detective. Why are you really here?"

"Because you pissed me off in a big way, Mr. King. I didn't need a wrinkled overcoat to understand you were hiding something." The detective's brown eyebrows met in the center. "By all accounts, you are an honorable man. I gave you every chance to come clean. Why wouldn't you tell me about Dalton's ugly fetish of stealing from the people he violated? I could have helped you find the duffle bags. You wouldn't have had to steal yellow pages from the library phone-books - another crime by the way."

"You have every reason to be upset with me," Jackson said. "Since we are being casual here, do you go by Lawrence or Larry?"

"For you, it's Detective Hill," he said in a stern voice. "Why, Mr. King?"

"Reason number one, Dalton Peppers' actions traumatized most of us in one way or another. If you had found all of the stolen items, how long would it take to release them to their rightful owner? And would it have been a priority for you and your department cronies to find the people Dalton victimized?" Jackson pushed a palm out. "A rhetorical question. It would take months or even years of bureaucracy for those items to be released. Who in your department would have been assigned the task of finding Dalton's victims?"

"You raised several good points, Mr. King. But the law says—"

"Mrs. Travers may never get over the trauma of what Dalton did to her as a child. Those frames in the pillowcase were a present from her beloved father and they represented a chance for Dani to move on with her life. What does the law say about that?"

Hill ran a hand across his crew cut. He stared out the apartment window.

"Another salient point, Mr. King. You said there were two reasons."

Jackson stood up and pointed to the cigar boxes. He waited until the detective motioned with an approving hand before picking up all three boxes and placing them onto the table.

"As you can see," Jackson swept a hand at the items on the floor, "almost everything Dalton swiped had no monetary value, including Mrs. Travers' frames."

The detective nodded. "Go on."

"Are you a baseball fan, detective?"

"I pitched for Sacramento State until I blew out my arm. Yes, I'm a big fan."

"Did you collect baseball cards as a kid?"

"Baseball and football cards. They're in a shoe box at my parents' house."

"What is the most valuable baseball card ever printed?"

"I read an article about that. It's the Honus Wagner card. He was a shortstop for the Pittsburgh Pirates way back when. I forget in what year or who manufactured the card."

"The American Tobacco Company printed the Honus Wagner card between 1909 and 1911. At today's 1994 price, it's worth close to a million. Would you care to see it?"

Hill stared at the box. "Are you shitting me? Hell yes."

Jackson untied the cord, opened the lid, and peeled away the wax paper. He pushed the box in front of the detective. A grunt of astonished air emitted from Hill's mouth as he ogled the card. He smiled, looked at Jackson, then back at Honus.

"Detective Hill, before you is the Holy Grail of baseball cards. I think of it as the Holy Honus. Shoeless Joe Jackson and Ty Cobb are underneath Honus, among other Hall of Fame greats. Mickey Mantle's rookie card is in another box. My whole collection is worth well over two million dollars." Jackson waited a few beats. "Now I ask you. Has anything ever been stolen or missing from your police evidence lockup?"

"Not often, but it has happened."

"I didn't want to take the chance," Jackson said. "Ninety-nine point nine percent of your fellow officers are honest, but all it would take is one knowledgeable bent blue ..."

Detective Hill rocked back and forth in the chair. Jackson was seeing another side of the stunned policeman. A human side he liked much better.

"As a boy," Jackson said, "all of the cards in these cigar boxes were my friends; my most prized possessions. I spent countless hours studying them; picturing them playing. To this day I can cite all of the stats and numbers on the back of the cards. They never held a dollar value for me. However, to this kid they were worth all the gold in Fort Knox."

"Okay," the detective said. "There's one thing I don't get. You told LeAnn and the Colfax storage managers you were planning to search for the people victimized by Peppers. Speaking as a cop, how in Babe Ruth's name could you possibly pull it off?"

"The idea came from Mrs. Travers. I know most billboard plant owners throughout the United States. We all have to do our share of PSA's - public service ads. Through trade and goodwill I can put out a well worded message in almost every state. I don't know how successful it would be, but I'd sure like to give it a shot."

"Mr. King."

"Yes, Detective Hill."

"Call me Larry. How can I help you with your venture?"

CHAPTER THIRTY-FIVE

Jackson entered the J King Outdoor building holding a large white box with red ribbon tied into a bow. He held Yogi's leash in his other hand. Rose approached Jackson with a concerned look on her face. He unsnapped the leash from Yogi's collar. The diminutive dog ran for his comfy zone underneath Jackson's desk like Yogi did every morning.

"I was worried about you, Jackson," she said. "You are always the first person here. And you didn't answer my calls yesterday afternoon."

"I'm sorry, Rose. Yesterday I was on the road and got involved in a heavy-duty discussion with a lawman. The cell phone reception probably would have been spotty at best. I had to put something in my safe deposit boxes at the bank this morning." He handed the white box to Rose. "Would you please send this to Dani?"

"No." Rose pushed the box back at Jackson. "Send it yourself."

Rose turned and walked away. Jackson peered up at the ceiling. Most likely, she was still upset with him about Dani leaving and going back to West Virginia. He understood Rose's resentment, but she had no idea how much Dani's absence was eating at him. Rose eventually might get over Dani's departure, but he wouldn't. If another employee had given him similar attitude, he would have dealt with him or her in a quick and sharp way. Rose, however, wasn't only an employee. She was a trusted friend and family; the only family he had left.

Jackson carried the box into his darkened office and placed it on the credenza. He reached into his pocket and put the metallic finished Sturdee Lock with an inserted gold key next to the box. He flipped up the light switch and noticed Yogi wasn't underneath his desk. Instead, the little traitor was in doggy seventh heaven lying on Dani's lap having his tummy and chest rubbed by the person he loved most.

Dani was wearing a blue pants suit and makeup, unlike the woman who had entered his office over a month ago. He could almost taste the adrenalin making his veins pulse. Even if he knew what to say, the lump in his throat would restrict his ability to speak.

"Well, at least Yogi is glad to see me," Dani said. "The shape of that lock and gold key looks familiar. Is that pretty box a present for a special woman in your life?"

Jackson cleared his throat; not once, but twice.

"As a matter of fact, it is," he said in a scratchy voice.

"Lucky girl. You must really love her."

"With all my heart."

"Do you know why I'm here?" she asked.

Whoa, a loaded question. Did Dani return to take Yogi back to West Virginia? Or maybe she came back to live with Rose. He shook his head.

"A promise is a promise, Jackson. I never told you what Dr. Seuss said."

"No, you didn't."

"If I tell what you what Dr. Seuss said, can I have the present?"

"Is this a negotiation, Mrs. Travers?"

"Yes, Mr. King. If I quote the Dr. Seuss maxim to you, I get the present and I also get to be your lover for as long as you want me."

"You drive a hard bargain, Mrs. Travers."

"I learned from the best." Dani stood and put Yogi on the chair. "I'm willing to up my offer to close the deal."

"I'm listening."

"I get the present and the rights to be your lover. In return you get the Dr. Seuss quote and a quote of my own."

"In order for me to agree, I would have to hear the quotes first," he demanded.

Dani moved to stand in front of Jackson and locked eyes with him.

"Dr. Seuss said, 'you know you're in love when you can't fall asleep because reality is finally better than your dreams.'" Dani inched closer to him. "I'm exhausted from lack of sleep, Jackson."

"That makes two of us, Dani. Dr. Seuss was a wise man. How could you ever top his saying?"

Dani clasped her hands around his neck. "If a woman can wake up each morning next to the man she loves, it's a dream come true."

"Deal!"

ACKNOWLEDGEMENTS

A heartfelt thank you to the following people for contributing, in a myriad of ways, to my novels *The Ticker, Will to Kill,* and *When the Enemy Is You.*

Debbie Aldred, Fred Aldred, Allison Anson, Ava Archibald, Bill Archibald, Bob Archibald, Julie Archibald, Nancy Archibald, Frank Baldwin (Author of *Balling the Jack & Jake & Mimi*)Alyn Beals, Scott Benner (Mayor of Bennerville), Elaine Blossom, Maria Bolleri, Ray Bolleri, Randal Brandt (The Bancroft Library at the University of California, Berkeley), Donna Smith Brown, Bill Burns, Barbara Butera, Frank Butera, Dennis Cacace, Carole Carl, Sharyl Carter, Danielle Carvalhaes, Sue Chamberlain, Shiela Cockshott, Carroll Collins III, Mary Ruth Conley, Al Connell, Raquel Cosare, Ryan Cosare, Diana Crosetti, Pat Cuendet (Author of *The Ghost In The Garden*), Brian Davis (Host of *Damn Good Movie Memories* - The Podcast), Darryl Davis, Gary Davis, Joanne Davis, Helen Dolan, Barbara Drotar (Author of *Searching For Sophia*), Carolyn Flohr, Don Flohr, Garrett, Gin Geraldi, Joni Gimnicher, Steve Gimnicher, Sue Goldman, Jeannie Graham, Margi Grant, Karen Griffiths, Barbara Hembey, Bill Hembey, Carol Henderson, Laurel Anne Hill (Author of *Heroes Arise & The Engine Woman's Light*), Ray Johnson, Mark Jones, Murray Kanefsky, Marie Kennedy, Julie Kosmides, Naty Kwan, Jennifer Lindsey, Kathy Love, Dr. Mike Ludovico, Serena Ludovico, Laura Lujan, Karin Marshall, Mike Marshall, Allison Martindale, Alicia Mazzoni, Jana McBurney-Lin (Author of *My Half of the Sky & Blossoms & Bayonets*), Sharen McConnell, Lorraine McGrath, Rockin' Roy McKinney, Tracy McNamara, Amanda McTigue (Author of *Going to Solace*), Princess Kristina Merlini, Virginia Messer, Kristol Miles, Gus Milon, Jeff Morena, Sue Murray, Colleen Conley Navarro, Dr. David Nichols, Bill Orrock, Beverly Paterson, Alicia Robertson, Ken Rolandelli, Lora Rolandelli, Debby Rose, Dr. Howard Rose, Martha Clark Scala (Author of *Assembling a Life: Claiming the Artist in My Father and Myself*), Seton Hospital Wound Care Staff, Elaine Silver, Scott Smith (Author of *The Ruins & A Simple Plan*), Dr. Kalpanu Srinivasan, Steve Stahl, Dr. Lisa Stiller, Kelli Jo Stratinsky, Rick Taylor, Scherrie Taylor, Scott Taylor, Steve Teani, Catherine Teitelbaum, Gail Tesi, Elizabeth Tuck, Bill Tyler, Marge Tyree, Pat Vitucci, Leslie Walsh, Vicki Williams, Bob Young, Rebecca Young, Donnalyn Zarzeczny, Joe Zukin.

*My apologies, in advance, if I omitted a deserving person's name.